PARABLES FROM OTHER PLANETS

BOOKS BY HUGH AND GAYLE PRATHER

A Book for Couples

Notes to Each Other

BOOKS BY HUGH PRATHER

Notes to Myself

Notes on Love and Courage

Notes on How to Live in the World . . .
    and Still Be Happy

The Quiet Answer

A Book of Games

There Is a Place Where
    You Are Not Alone

I Touch the Earth,
    the Earth Touches Me

PARABLES

from OTHER

PLANETS

Folktales of the Universe

HUGH PRATHER

AND

GAYLE PRATHER

Illustrations by Stacey Smith

BANTAM BOOKS

New York   Toronto   London   Sydney   Auckland

PARABLES FROM OTHER PLANETS

A BANTAM BOOK / DECEMBER 1991

Illustrations by Stacey Smith.

Library of Congress Cataloging-in-Publication Data

Prather, Hugh.
  Parables from other planets : folktales of the universe / Hugh
and Gayle Prather.
    p.   cm.
  ISBN 0-553-07251-X
  1. Fantastic fiction, American.   I. Prather, Gayle.   II. Title.
PS3566.R27P37   1991
813'.54—dc20   91-13146
                                                           CIP

Published simultaneously in the United States and Canada

Bantam Books are published by Bantam Books, a division of
Bantam Doubleday Dell Publishing Group, Inc. Its trademark,
consisting of the words "Bantam Books" and the portrayal of a
rooster, is Registered in U. S. Patent and Trademark Office and
in other countries. Marca Registrada. Bantam Books, 666 Fifth
Avenue, New York, New York 10103.

Printed in the United States of America

BVG   0   9   8   7   6   5   4   3   2   1

Contents

Prologue

Gayle and I were recently in Patagonia (the real Patagonia, southeast of Tucson), taking a taxi from the Museum of the Horse to Red Mountain Produce and Crystals, when the driver started leading the conversation in an unexpected direction.

"You guys writers?"

"How did you know?"

"You're both wearing tweed jackets and smoking pipes."

He looked in the rearview mirror for an answer, but got only stunned silence, and probably saw us edging out of his view. "What I mean is your ethereal bodies have tweed jackets. The pipes I got through E.O.P.—extraolfactory perception."

"What a relief; for a second there we thought you were crazy."

"No, I'm just psychic. Of course writers don't smoke pipes anymore, but the archetypes of the collective unconscious are immune to health fads." He glanced at me in the mirror to see if we were impressed. "I do readings and charts. I only drive a cab as sort of a laboratory of life. Take this guy I had in here about a month ago . . ." He looked back for encouragement. Evidently our silence was enough. "Guy says he's here from the island universe of Mervin. Said he was completing his assignment. He left this manuscript that's supposed to tell all about his "quest," but not everyone can read it. I can't make anything of it, but he said the writer who was supposed to translate it would be able to read it quite easily."

He handed back a common-enough-looking blue folder, a little thinner, perhaps, than a full-length book, and when we first looked at the text it seemed fuzzy, like the dot matrix used to list illegibly the ingredients on packages of supermarket pastries. Although not written in any language we knew, we noticed that by staring at it, a kind of meaning began to emerge. Startled, Gayle slapped it shut. I said, in a voice that came out louder than I had intended, "Well, I guess that eliminates us. We're *two* writers, not one."

He evidently didn't hear me well because he said into the mirror, "Yeah, I had a feeling you guys were the ones."

We soon found that it was going to be easier to take it with us than argue with him, so, blue folder in hand, we exited the cab as quickly as possible when he stopped in front of Red Mountain, and I handed him the money through the window.

This strange little man refused both the fare or a tip, saying that he had been feeling too much responsibility for the past month and was grateful just to have the thing off his hands.

When we looked back, the taxi had disappeared. Inside Red Mountain we told our story to Barry and Annie, who had owned the store for many years. They reminded us that Patagonia had never had a cab company. The town is only one mile long.

PARABLES FROM OTHER PLANETS

My Record of Lights
in Other Places

To my readers on Earth:
My name is unimportant because I, like you, am merely
a child who once lost his way. My teacher is Mervin,
who manifests himself as the third universe of the Hexa-
hedron. Mervin delights in giving assignments to those of
us who still think we need to experience life more fully.
Because I had a trace of this need myself, he suggested
that I undertake a journey, but before he explained what
it was, he said, "I know what you want and I am committed to giving it to you. However, you think that what
you want is a quest. And a quest you shall be given, one
that may also help others who yearn for experience. But
like all things you seek outside yourself, this quest will
merely be the package I wrap around the one true gift
you long to give and therefore already have. In all that I
say and do, I will never deceive you, but since I know
your heart better than you, I will trick you a little whenever I can." He then giggled so hard that tiny changes
could be detected in the magnetic fields of his solar systems by some of the more receptive beings therein, who
suddenly found themselves in a state of bliss.

"Your assignment is to answer the question: Is any
part of truth now absent within the cosmos? The children
of God think that they have lost truth, but they have only
scattered it. Therefore, you are to visit each inhabited

planet and discover which aspects of truth have been denied and which are beginning to be recognized. When you have completed this assignment, return to each planet and leave a record of the fruits of your mission. This record will be yet another reminder of what has been forgotten but not lost. The only thing that the children of God have yet to do is choose to remember what is already in their hearts."

Having completed my journey through the cosmos, I now leave with you this record of lights in other places. Although merely a small sampling edited for the peoples of Earth, these sayings and tales are an adequate answer to the question that haunts the children of the universe, no matter where they may be found.

Ending the Dream

The town of Vaduz is nestled within the Great Bridge that spans the binary planets of Orb and Bex. This natural land bridge or Fusion supports the numerous thoroughfares connecting the planets, and the most popular vehicle is very similar to the automobiles seen on Earth, with an added air-cushion generator that allows the cars to plane at higher velocities.

There was once a mother living in Vaduz who discovered that she could enter her son's dreams at will. One night the child began thrashing in his sleep. Instantly the mother saw that her son was in a driverless car that was speeding out of control. She closed her eyes and started to enter his dream, but suddenly she stopped. Many times before she had made the changes in his dreams that she had thought he would want, but the dreams had always turned again to discord. She knew that she had the ability to apply the brake and stop the car, but being wiser now she saw that a disturbed dream is caused by a disturbed dreamer, and no matter how it is altered, it cannot reflect more peace than the dreamer himself possesses. Wanting now only to bring peace to his mind, she lifted her son up. In the dream the car flew off the road and started falling. She held her son securely in her arms. In the dream he saw the walls of the car closing in. She sang a lullaby of her love and of her son's eternal safety. In the dream he saw the choir start to sing at his own funeral. Yet slowly the child began to feel the warm presence of his mother enfolding him, and as he awoke to the reality of her love, his dream ended.

Did you will your child's nightmare? Certainly not! And are you not the child of your *divine* Mother? Therefore it should not discourage you to recognize that the Divine did not create the world as you see it. When you deny the nightmarish nature of the world, you merely fight with your own mind. And when you ask Love to change worldly circumstances, you are asking The One Who Knows You to ensure that you continue dreaming. Love does not intervene in your life because Love knows your deeper request: that your pain end and that you see your fellow travelers as they truly are. This is why your Mother holds you in her arms and smiles gently at all your imaginings and at your many requests that one illusion be exchanged for another. She loves you too much to intervene. She merely waits for you to remember who you are, and while she waits she sings to you of the beauties of your Home, the wonders of your day, and of your oneness with all that is bright and eternal.

How do you escape from this nightmare of chaos and calamity you call Earth? How do you look beyond a world of separate snapping egos, of fading sunsets and passing pleasantries, of beauty that cannot heal, of love that ends, of success that fades? How do you look through to the living breath of every creature great or small? How do you know them all in innocence? How do you walk the ground that cannot crumble? How do you find peace that cannot end? How do you awake?

You laugh, O child of God. You relax your mind into a smile.

The Book

There was born, on the vast and verdant moon of Unah, a child who came from his mother's womb holding a small book in his arms. Whenever anyone would attempt to remove the book, the infant would cry so loudly that the pain of the sound would force even the deaf to desist. The child grew up to become the great prophet Sirna, and the book became the holy scripture of the land.

One day two of Sirna's students approached the master and said, "There is much in The Book over which we contend, and after many months of discussion we are unable to resolve our differences. Would you, Master, hear our dispute and give us the answers we need?"

Sirna looked up and said, "Do you see the goat on the hill before us? Go and give the goat The Book and he will answer the dispute."

The students were appalled. "But, Master," they said, "if we give The Book to the goat, he will eat it."

Sirna answered, "It is better that The Book make a goat happy than come between any two people."

Master Sirna and his goat meditate by the lake

Procession of Beggars

On the little planet of Qwa-Megambatu there is a three-day holy season that comes at the beginning of Planting. It is the tradition that all beggars of the land and any who wish to join them, rich and poor alike, come into the villages and on the third day form a procession. At the rising of the second or midday sun, they walk down the streets, and as they pass, children run from their homes and pick one person out of the many to present with a gift.

This tradition had its inception at a time when the little village of Qwa-Sii was in bitter turmoil over issues concerning the village's chronic poverty. The Holy One, disguised as a filthy, diseased beggar, came down from the mountains and walked among the people searching for anyone who still had the capacity to see goodness. All turned from him in disgust until the third day, when a young girl ran up to him and gave him her necklace of precious stones. She was an orphan who was passed between homes and the necklace was the only thing she owned that had belonged to her parents. When the villagers asked her why she had given such a cherished gift to a beggar, she answered, "Because I saw in his eyes the peace that we have all denied."

From that time on, so pleasant was the atmosphere of the village that it eventually became known as Qwa-Kata or "joy of Qwa." As more and more visitors came to Qwa-Kata, and its businesses flourished, to protect their newly found prosperity, the citizens began the annual tradition called The Procession of Beggars. However, after several years the village had again slipped back into its same rancorous and miserable state, this time over issues about money.

Again The Holy One came, disguised this time as a wealthy merchant dressed in a splendid white garment and a jeweled cape, and walked through the streets searching for anyone who could see his purity. For three days the villagers turned from him in envy and suspicion, but on the third day, just as he was leaving, a boy playing in the ditch beside the road, sifting water and dust with his toy cups, asked the merchant if he would like to sit with him and share his cups.

For several hours the merchant and the child played together, and when the merchant finally left he was covered with mud. Several of the villagers had witnessed this strange sight and when they approached the boy to find out who the stranger was, they saw these words scratched in the ground: "It is not by giving jewels to beggars or mud to merchants that your village will know peace, but by giving the gift of an innocent vision to everyone you see."

And that is why today, when a child gives his gift to the person he has chosen in The Procession of Beggars, that person says to the child, "Thank you for recognizing who I am."

Too little provocation can lead to good temper.

PLANET: Cilcylon

TRANSLATION: A larger planet is locked in synchronous orbit between Cilcylon and its sun, eternally blocking direct sunlight. Cilcylon, however, is softly illuminated by eight moons that make its landscape of white sand one of the loveliest and most peaceful in the universe. It is as if the people of Cilcylon have derived their wisdom from their surroundings, because their gentle teaching is always of stillness in some form. They lead simple, contemplative lives, and, when asked, often counsel visitors to avoid engaging in useless battles. **"A mind that jumps around grows smaller,"** they say.

MEANING: Whenever possible, avoid those things that call to your ego. Cilcylon is often used as a retreat, for here the disturbing stimuli have been reduced to the point where the seed of one's serenity can begin to grow. Referring, perhaps, to the fact that soft footsteps are needed to reach the top of a towering Cilcylon sand dune, there is also this kindred saying: **Only a tranquil spirit can see beyond itself.**

Induriti blesses the derelict

Induriti and the Splendor

Induriti and her students were walking through the village of Darseth when a derelict called out, "You who worship the Splendor! The Splendor is the leavings of a groattoad!" Induriti stopped and gave the man her blessing, and then walked on.

Immediately her students began remonstrating with her: "Teacher, it is written that no one shall curse the Splendor and live, and yet you passed by without even a rebuke."

Induriti answered, "Is not the Splendor all-powerful, the supreme Beauty, the artisan of all that really is? Surely It does not need our protection."

Still her students persisted, "But it is part of your vows to uphold the holy laws. Have you not broken your vows?"

"My vow, my pleasure, and my life," answered Induriti, "is to understand others as the Splendor understands us. This derelict's curse was a plea that we notice him. If a man is drowning, does it matter how his cry for help is worded?"

Still her students were not satisfied. "But could you not have demanded that the Splendor be honored, as well as have stopped to bless?"

Induriti seated herself on a stone. She closed her eyes, and when she opened them she looked first at the gold horizon of the planet Lolona. In stillness it encircled them like the trail of a comet. "O students of Beauty," she said, "this curse that you fret so much over has long since died on the lips of the derelict. The only place it continues to be honored is in your minds."

The Last Wolf

Mashesta could not understand why he had been chosen to kill the last wolf. He was not yet a grown man. It was not fair. But Cintosh had called him before the Council and told him he must do it. Cintosh, who had tried to save the wolves, who had spoken interminably about the need for wolves. Cintosh the ancient, Cintosh the forgetful, Cintosh the obtuse.

Mashesta packed lightly. This should not be too difficult. The last wolf was old now. It should not take him more than a few days to track it down and shoot it. He hated what was left of the forest. Another of Cintosh's pets—the forest. Mashesta looked forward to the day when the old man died and progress could be resumed.

The diffused light of the forest always bothered Mashesta, as if shadows from some netherworld still existed there. But the netherworld had been banished years ago. It no longer existed except in the minds of a few old men. And perhaps in the mind of one old wolf.

For three days now Mashesta had caught glimpses of the wolf, but just as he sighted with his rifle, the wolf would disappear. The third night he camped near a pond, and, watching the embers of his fire, he seemed to drift off to sleep, for suddenly, whether in dream or in fact, the wolf came into the clearing. It stood before him, its eyes boring into his, and then it spoke.

"So, Mashesta, you have come to kill me. I am ready to die, but not die from a distance at the cold hands of that insentient stick. It is the weapon of a coward. If you are to take me, it must be fang against fang, blood against blood, strength against strength."

"Why are you ready to *die?*" asked Mashesta.

As if not hearing him, the wolf continued. "Not only must you kill me in this way, but you must also cut out my heart while it still beats and devour it. Our blood must mingle, our breath must fill each other's lungs. Only then will I die. And only then will you truly live."

"You are trying to trick me," answered Mashesta. "You would easily defeat me in that kind of fight."

"You have your knife. That is sufficient, for I repeat to you that I am ready to die. I am alone here. I have no fear of death, but I do have a love of this forest. I would leave it my grandeur and my freedom."

"I am not the one to do this thing," pleaded Mashesta.

"But you are the one who is here; therefore you are the one. There still beats within your heart the remembrance of the wild, the unattached, the unquenched. And you must not let it die. For if you do, man will continue to feed upon his own soul as well as the souls of others."

"Then why don't I let you live and return to my village and say that I could not find you. I could say that you are already dead."

"Then you would live and die with deceit. This moment is not an accident. Why do you think the wolves have been killed? Because they interfered with man's plans for the wilderness? No! They have been killed because they reminded men of that which was noble, that which was free, that which could not be bought and paid for. You need me more than I need you. But because this is the land of my ancestors, I offer you this gift: my heart, which will unite with yours and lead you away from the awful numbness of what you call progress. But if you stand apart from me and kill me from the distance that you believe separates us, then man will never again know what it feels like to ride the wild winds of passion. Not the passion of the flesh, for that he has ridden too long, but the passion of a soul that honors its roots in wilderness.''

"I cannot possibly do this. I am afraid to fight with hands that have no claws, with a mouth that has no fangs. A mere knife does not make up for this.''

"Yet *I* am not afraid,'' said the wolf, "and it is I who must die.''

"But the outcome is not certain. You might kill me. Why should I trust you?''

"This is what you do not yet understand,'' said the wolf. "You think that to have no attachments is to be uncommitted. You think that to embrace the wilderness is to be unprincipled. Yet, unlike men, a wolf has honor. He cares for his young and never abandons his mate. To protect his pack, he will lay down not only his self-interests but his life.''

Mashesta woke before dawn, strangely disturbed, and as he stirred the coals of his night's fire, he vowed to find the wolf and shoot it before the day ended. There was something about this task that made him want to complete it and return to civilization quickly.

It was near the pond that Mashesta saw it. Larger than he had imagined, covered in the matted fur of one who has too long lived alone. And it was still. Mashesta raised his rifle and brought the wolf into his sights. The wolf was watching him, he could feel its eyes looking fearlessly into the barrel of his weapon. He longed to pull the trigger and be done with this deed. To carry the wolf's carcass back to the village in triumph. To resume his real life.

But he could not fire, and the wolf began to advance upon him. He felt sweat break out over his brow. His heart battered his chest like a caged enemy. His breath sawed through his mouth with the hard bursts of air that do not replenish the lungs. At the last moment, before the wolf sprang, Mashesta threw down his rifle, unsheathed his knife, and, with the scream of one who acts from long acquaintance with his limitations, leaped and met the wolf in midair.

At the start there seemed no hope that Mashesta would emerge victorious, that he would do no more than die ignominiously under the fangs of this beast. But somehow the wolf's mouth never reached his vitals. And gradually Mashesta sensed a weariness in the wolf and a strength in himself that he had not felt before. Now he fought with renewed courage, or rather, with new courage, for he had never experienced this emotion. He did not hate the wolf, rather he hated his own timidity, and as he drove his knife deep into the wolf's throat and severed its lines of breath, he breathed in the intoxicating air of fearlessness. Without thinking, as the wolf twitched in death, Mashesta cut open its chest and tore its heart from its body and thrust it into his own mouth. Blood poured from his lips, from his wounds, and from the wounds of the wolf. There was hair in his nostrils, in his mouth, in his belly.

Mashesta stood for a moment trembling, not with fear, but with knowledge. He stumbled to the pond and threw himself into its icy depths. And when he emerged he was whole. For a long while he stood looking at the body of the wolf. He no longer needed to carry it triumphantly back to the village to prove his manhood and his courage. In fact he now realized that to treat the wolf in this manner would be to degrade it and dishonor the lesson it had taught. Mashesta did not have the implements to dig a grave and knew that the wolf had no need of burial, but he lifted the body and carried it to a place within the bosom of the trees that he knew the wolf had loved. Then he laid it gently on the ground and covered it with leaves and with the soft vegetation of the forest floor.

When he returned to the village, Mashesta spoke to no one, but went directly to Cintosh. He stood quietly before his ancient leader and smiled with great affection. "Cintosh, father of our welfare," he said, "you will be happy to know that the wolves will live forever."

**What will the future hold for you?
Only the love you give today.**

PLANET: (name unknown)

TRANSLATION AND MEANING: The only recognizable
   artifact on this abandoned world is the above
   message, carved in huge furrows on the planet's
   desiccated and ruined surface.

Dancing Arrow

This fragment is all that remains of what is believed to be the last interview with Saguano, called by many on the planet of Iom the "dancing arrow," because of his unequivocal philosophy and joyous temperament. Oddly, Saguano granted this interview to The Disbeliever, *a small periodical that throughout its publishing history had harshly attacked Saguano and his followers.*

TD: The facts of your life are widely known: how you were a common farmer married to a local woman who bore you seven daughters, how you sought for no more than the warm winds and rains to nurture your crops and then how, during The War, just before you returned home, your wife and daughters were tortured and brutally slaughtered, even the youngest, who was only seven years old. My question to you is this: If you had really loved them, how could you have come home to that gruesome scene and then spent the rest of your life teaching the importance of understanding and even of humor?

SAGUANO: Would the crime have offended you less, and would you have thought that I had loved my family more, if it had not been brutal, if only my wife and elder daughters had been killed, and if they had been quickly shot but not beaten? Are you surprised that I chose not to extend the same anger that killed them?

TD: You found them that day—tortured, having spent their final hours in agony—and what did you think, that your God had honored them by wanting them with him? Or that his divine plan was to spare you?

SAGUANO: No, that day I believed that I had been cursed by God.

TD: Yet you are still smiling. Haven't you taught this planet to forsake vengeance so that you can continue to deny what happened to you? You don't seem to recognize that your teachings have placed many people in grave danger.

SAGUANO: My son, I have simply tried to give to others what saved me from overwhelming pain. I never asked for a follower.

TD: But all examples teach and everyone is a teacher. The effect of your conspicuous example is that most people now will not fight back. You have eliminated war but not aggression.

SAGUANO: Yes. And perhaps that is not entirely good. Evil must be resisted and it is extremely difficult to see how to do this in each situation. Kind does not mean weak, and I have never taught martyrdom. I only know that to take hate personally—that is, to take it into my heart and see the attacker with the same eyes with which he sees me—is to inflict pain on myself and to extend the world's ancient wound. I could have spent my life hunting down the attackers and killing them one by one. Indeed, as I laid my beloved wife and children into their graves, as I covered their faces with cold earth, I was consumed with just this thought.

TD: Anyone would be. It's right to be consumed with hatred in such circumstances.

SAGUANO: It is certainly not wrong to feel this way—but how could hatred have made the situation better? Would it have assuaged my sorrow? Would it have honored my loved ones? And if I had followed its leadings, would it have set for me a constructive destiny?

TD: Revenge is natural. It is a form of control. It is an inherent emotion that marshals our defensive energies. You would have served justice and your family better by seeing to it that these savages never did this to anyone else. As it is, your family has died a meaningless death. Evil must be punished and eradicated by everyone who can reach it.

SAGUANO: Attack simply fans the fires of counterattack. If the evildoer is struck down in anger, another rises to take his place. It is good to bring criminals to justice, and there are those who are well equipped to do this with fairness. However, pursuing my enemies is not my function in life. I did not want to extend my pain. I did not want one mother or father of the attackers to experience my suffering. And if I had sought to punish, where would the punishment have stopped?

TD: With those who committed the crime, of course.

SAGUANO: And what of those who drove them to this act of depravity, and those who in turn drove them? We are all connected, you see, and we can no longer deny this connection. My choice, as I began to recover a little from the death of all that I had ever loved, was to remain eternally damaged, the living proof of their guilt, or to rise out of it and shake the anger from me. Do not forget that it took me many years to accomplish this, and certainly no one is to be condemned if it takes them even longer. And I will admit to you one other thing: it is equally difficult for me to respond to the hundreds of *little* provocations that arise every day, to respond, that is, from something within me besides irritation.

TD: Let us turn from your tragedy—which you have already dealt with in your own peculiar way—to the tragedy of others. You have said before that "laughter is the loveliest sound on the planet," that "humor is vision," that "a laughing heart accomplishes all," and other such pronouncements. However, *your* pain came from your association with, your connection to, the far greater pain of your family. You did not experience what they did. What of the millions of others who suffer directly? Are these people to laugh also?

SAGUANO: One who is truly laughing is *never* laughing at horror. To do so would be heartless. Instead, he is laughing in oneness with what he sees beyond horror. Such laughter really never ends. One does not mock or even slight another's pain. One should not even question another's fears. Laughter is merely the happy and often silent recognition of what could help and of how it will all turn out someday. It extends a hand into the waters of pain but remains standing on firm ground.

TD: Seriousness and realism have accomplished far more for society than laughter. In fact, aside from a temporary lifting of spirits, not one historical change can be attributed to laughter.

SAGUANO: You of course are right. And the reason is that it has never been tried. And yet, for all the humorless changes we have had, is our world really any different from what it has always been?

A Planet Named Sue

There was once a planet named Sue that had almost everything. It had all the biologically important molecules. It had all the essential gases. It had an atmosphere with abundant water vapor. And it had already advanced through the stages of prebiotic synthesis of organic matter. It even had lightning and just the right amount of ultraviolet radiation from its sun. But it did not have life. Nothing moved except the winds. Nothing wept except the clouds.

As modern astrometaphysics has discovered, planets are conscious entities, albeit rather passive ones. Passivity, however, was not one of Sue's shortcomings. For a planet she was very active, especially in pursuing her one great dream, to be a planet that supported life. Sue fantasized about great birdlike beasts rising like winged moons from her oceans, and whalelike things blowing columns of lambent water into the air. She could almost feel tiny shelled and scaly creatures waddling and scurrying up her shores and digging moist nests in her rivers. She imagined a thousand—no, ten thousand—birdsongs caroled from the trees. And at night, it was as if she could already hear insects making fiddles and drums out of their hairy legs. But then the illusion would end and there would be no real sound, only the deceitful sound of lifeless waves breaking over inorganic shores and pol-

A heart takes root on the planet of Sue

lenless winds blowing over a plantless terrain. And her longing would return.

Sue knew that if just one lost astronaut were to step out of his capsule for a stretch, and a little dander would drop to the ground, or a loose hair teeming with microbes (normal ones, of course), she would be in business. Or if a stray asteroid or two were to break open their treasure of carbonaceous chrondrites and a few select amino acids were to settle into her primordial dust, perhaps she could unite them with an earthquake, water them with a cloudburst, and fuse them with a lightning bolt—then maybe something would begin to move.

So, toward these ends, and toward every other life-bringing scenario she could imagine, Sue bent her efforts. Whenever she saw spaceships, she varied her mass and produced attention-getting orbits. She focused her gravitational waves toward any passing comet or bevy of meteoroids. Through tiny implosions on her surface, she banged out interestingly spaced electromagnetic vibrations toward far-off terrestrial radio-telescopes. But nothing worked, and soon Sue became depressed.

A depressed planet is not a happy thing to see, but since there was no one to witness her state, perhaps it doesn't matter that Sue's depression lasted ten million, seven hundred and two years. It ended a short time after she noticed a self-help satellite heading toward her from intergalactic space. Somehow the satellite had wandered from its orbit within a dG2 solar system near the Orion Arm, and it wasn't long before it took up orbit around Sue.

Evidently the message it beamed had gotten stuck at just one thought, which the Reverend Applegate repeated endlessly. In a clear, confident tone he said, "All you will ever need is within you now."

At first Sue assumed that he was talking about some well-stocked thing like a beehive or a wintering ant colony. But his use of the word *you* did bother her. Surely his message had not been meant for the ears of insects, unless, of course, they ruled the planet he came from, but if so, why would a noninsect presume to advise them? Although she was resistant to the idea (because Sue was certainly not New Age), she began to wonder if the satellite was a sign. Satellites were not supposed to break out of solar systems, and laser recordings were not supposed to get stuck.

If the message was now meant for her, everything she needed to produce life was within her. But this made no sense. To get at her nickel-iron and sulfur core and her primary and parental magmas, she would have to turn herself inside out, and this would destroy her. Sue was tempted to indulge in another million or two years of depression.

But the Reverend Applegate would not let up, and Sue was reluctant to create a stratospheric storm that would blow him on his way. After all, this was the first company she had ever had, and what if he *was* a sign? So Sue decided to use her mind instead of letting it use her. She listened intently to the message.

The message, she realized, did *not* imply, "All you will ever need—in order to get what else you want—is within you now." Nor did it say which "you" the "all" was within. She had all she needed in her atmosphere, her crust, and her Moho to make life, and yet she had no life. No, that was not entirely true. She had *her* life.

Now there was something to think about.

What did life mean? Well, she had consciousness, she had awareness, she had mind. And the whole universe was *in* her mind. There it was, all its particle clouds and pulsars and supernovas, all its nebulas and quasars and white dwarfs, all its comets and constellations and regular and irregular galaxies. And she was part of it all.

Suddenly Sue broke into song. She had everything, she had *life*.

But then she remembered. And her singing stopped. Her *planetary body* did not have everything.

As if an echo, her song now came back to her, and she heard the lyrics she herself had been singing: "Life is more important than the body that has it on loan."

A few solar revolutions later, Sue was so busy being happy that it was a moment or two before she realized that the Reverend Applegate had stopped talking. When she looked up she saw the reason. Three spacebirds sat on the satellite's solar panel, and she was tempted to again become morose. Here were these lonely, little-seen birds of the universe, creatures that had no home except an occasional asteroid, so ugly that other planets ran them off, birds that fed on nothing but granitic particles and water. . . .

"But my surface is ninety percent granite," Sue thought. "And I have all the water any bird could ever want."

And thus it was that Sue became the first wildlife refuge for spacebirds, creatures that visitors said somehow seemed different on her largely edible crust. Sue has recently been awarded an historical marker and is said to be very content.

Anyone can be happy for the space of one breath.

PLANET: Eusserwar

TRANSLATION: Besides Earth, this is one of the few planets where the most intelligent life forms live in the ocean. A "breath," therefore, takes in one's situation in a more literal sense.

MEANING: It's not life, but how life strikes you, that determines your happiness. Anyone can decide to be happy for one moment. The corollary of this saying addresses the question of permanent happiness: **Anyone can breathe more than once.** A fish lives in water, moves in water, breathes water, and is composed mostly of water. It is perhaps easier, therefore, for a fish to recognize that one's attitude toward what is out is one's attitude toward what is in. Thus the importance of acceptance. Or, as another Eusserwarian saying puts it: **Let it pass through you like water through your gills.**

Not Two Minds

The Bydersee solar system was once watched over by an unascended master named Pirs, who was a little disorganized but whose heart was in the right place. His most loyal student was Orky St'aussel, who lived on the planet Atnor-B. Orky had every worldly condition favorable to happiness: He had an ordinary face and body, a kind and average-looking wife, good-natured children unpossessed of genius, a steady paycheck from a nonwar industry, and he lived in a house that had not been overly landscaped. In short, Orky St'aussel had the greatest gift that his or any other world can offer: simplicity. And he had taken advantage of his circumstances by devoting himself deeply to Pirs's widely ignored philosophy termed Not Two Minds. (Pirs had always meant to give his teaching a more positive and informative title but had not yet gotten around to it.)

Orky's favorite NTM concept was: "The mind is like the sun: it gives the deepest tan to the objects it shines on the most." Pirs had highlighted the implications by adding this advice: "Therefore, be careful what paint you put in your paint gun because that will be the color of your walls."

Orky had never put neglect into his paint gun and as a result his family and close associates shone brightly with only the hues of laughter, grace, and lavish attention, so brightly, in fact, that they attracted the attention of the dark-hearted Nas Rugt, who controlled the neighboring solar system.

"The only reason that Orky St'aussel remains your loyal student," he said to Pirs, "is that you have put a protective hedge of commonness around him and his household. Let me upgrade everything Orky has and he will quickly forget you and your silly Not Two Minds philosophy."

"Very well," said Pirs, "you are free to give Orky a special life, but only on the condition that you lay not a finger on him personally."

Soon thereafter a neighbor came to Orky and said, "Did you know that the school took all the kids to the set of a game show today and that your children guessed the correct price of the Presidential Mansion that is being sold off as part of the new administration's austerity program? It comes with a hundred and twenty-six servants. Already the kitchen staff is impatiently awaiting your meal orders for the day, the gardeners want the list of autumn plants to be rotated, and you have thirteen employee disputes to settle among the housekeeping staff."

Shortly another neighbor came to Orky and said, "Did you know that the company you work for is the victim of a leveraged takeover and the new owner's psychic adviser has said that your name is the only one that is numerologically correct? You have been appointed the new board chairman and waiting in your office are the representatives of thirty-two charities, six consumer-advocate groups, and a tax auditor."

Soon another neighbor arrived and said, "Did you know that your wife got a coupon in the mail and took it in this morning to Honso, the great plastic surgeon? After the operation, Honso announced to the press that your wife is his masterpiece. You will not be able to go anywhere without men staring at her and gum companies offering her commercials to chew in a bathing suit."

Hearing all this, Orky fell to the ground and cried out to Pirs, "Master, I have been plagued with a fortune, an estate, and a beautiful wife, yet you have not intervened on my behalf. Being the originator of the great Not Two Minds philosophy, I trust your wisdom in this matter." And despite his many burdens, Orky did not turn from the teachings of Pirs.

Seeing the strength of Orky's devotion, Nas Rugt returned to Pirs and said, "It is true that your student Orky has remained loyal, but many can endure a charmed life as long as their body is ordinary. Let me transform his very flesh and you will see how superficial is Orky's commitment."

"Very well," said Pirs. "Provided you do not take his life, you may give Orky a special body."

Thus it came to pass that Orky's wife grew discontent with her husband's appearance, thinking it unworthy of her, and so began mixing hormones into his daily meals. Soon Orky had the face and physique of a god. Women started throwing themselves at him, magazines put him on their "Ten Married Men Most Likely To" lists, and political parties began noticing that he was tall enough to look presidential. As a consequence Orky's days were now consumed with press conferences to deny rumors that he was running for political office and with magazine interviews to deny rumors of what, as a married man, he was "most likely" to do. In the evenings, friends came to comfort him and ended up in protracted disagreements over the metaphysical implications of Orky's plight.

Through all of this Orky never wavered in his devotion to Not Two Minds. Nas Rugt, seeing that the grounds for Orky's steadfastness were more powerful than anything he had ever encountered, not only stopped suggesting new ways of testing Orky's faith but himself became a disciple.

In honor of his example, Pirs appeared before Orky and said, "Whenever anyone seeks an extreme condition within his world, whether it be an extreme in health, wealth, beauty, or power, he attracts the attention of the world and draws down upon himself its full range of emotions—emotions both desirable and undesirable. Not only have you not sought to set yourself apart, but when events elevated you and yours above all others, you did not give faith to this picture of a separate mind. Even though you have demonstrated that you do not need it in order to progress, so that your way might be a little easier, I will restore to you your full ordinariness: Your wife will become plain, your company will lose its numerologist, your children will no longer be lucky, a new administration will reclaim the Presidential Mansion, and your body will henceforth pass unnoticed in a crowd. More than this no man could desire."

The Innocence of Boats

Compared to the Earth's sun, Zui 3 is very large, giving off more than a hundred times the light and heat. However, the orbit of Yadonasora is sufficiently removed that the planet is eminently habitable. The two seasons of its solar year, which is approximately twenty-eight Earth years long, trigger an unusual water cycle below the planet's surface. As the cooler season begins, water rises from thousands of spout holes and Yadonasora becomes all ocean. During the warm season the planet returns to a predominantly dry-land state. Yadonasora's sage and adviser is So-To-Lo-Cho, Jewel of the Twinkling Planet, who is reputedly five and a half. As would be expected, many of his sayings involve boats, of which there are far more than people.

One day a man named Pe-Te-Leet came seeking help with his moodiness.

"Give me an example of this 'moodiness,' " said Cho.

"No one looks where he's going," said Leet. "Last night a family in a swamp boat almost ran into us. I stood on our bow and watched for twenty harsecs as the helmsman, a doddering three-year-old, left and returned to his post six times. He didn't even seem to notice us, and at the last moment I had to turn to avoid him. I, of course, became furious."

"Of course," said Cho, and fell silent.

The coming of the waters on Yadonasora

"But what can I do about my anger?"

"You can do nothing," said Cho, "because you believe that your anger is caused." And again he fell silent.

"But, O Jewel of the Twinkling Planet, surely there is something I can do. Not all men are as volatile as I."

"You could escape from your moods only if they were *not* caused. Do you not see that the three-year-old did not *cause* you to become angry?"

"But his swamp boat almost drifted into us. My whole family could have perished as a result of his negligence."

Cho smiled and gently placed his hand on Leet's arm. "My friend, are there not many abandoned boats on the ocean? If from your bow you had noticed that the boat was empty, and yet it had drifted toward you in exactly the same manner, what would you have done?"

"I would have turned out of its way."

"And would you have been angry?"

"No, it couldn't have helped doing what it did."

"Ah!" said Cho. "Boats are innocent! You give the most important gift of all to a mere boat. And yet boats are not even your brothers and sisters.

"Your anger came not from the boat almost ramming you, but from the fact that it was occupied by a living soul. You know that empty boats cannot help what they do, and yet you believe that people can. Last night, *you* could not have helped getting angry. But now that you are no longer empty, you have a choice."

**Being imperfect learning devices,
mistakes must be repeated.
Being imperfect learning devices,
mistakes must be repeated.**

PLANET: Nor

TRANSLATION AND MEANING: This thought was so widely practiced by the inhabitants of Nor that Nor no longer exists.

The Noarfians

Certainly one of the friendliest and most tolerant places
in the cosmos is the planet Noarf, which is ruled by
deeply intelligent beings remarkable for their rather large
red tongues, used not only in all the ways tongues are
usually used, but also in their greeting ritual. Perhaps it
is because the greeting remains on the face for a short
while as a moist reminder, that one feels such intimate
and long-lasting acceptance. Despite the many wet faces
(Noarfians greet after even very short absences and may
repeat their greeting several times during the course of
contact with another life form), there is very little infec-
tious disease on Noarf, except among the primary pets of
most families, creatures known as vexes, who are as
querulous, intolerant, and disloyal as the Noarfians are
the opposite. In fact, the question so frequently asked by
tourists is why do Noarfians keep such moody pets in
their homes, that a segment has been added to the program on the information holoscreen at the central space-
port, describing to newcomers the good points of the vex
and the advantages of this traditional relationship.
Nevertheless, many tourists leave the planet still shaking
their heads over this curious aspect of Noarfian culture.

The purpose of the holoscreen segment is not commercial, for no Noarfian family would think of selling
their vexes. It is simply another example of the inherent

kindness of the Noarfians. They do not want even vexes to be thought poorly of, although it is obvious to most that, except for their inventiveness and keen intelligence, there is little to recommend them. And even their intelligence, which on most planets would be considered extraordinary for a pet, is not the deep intelligence of the Noarfian, since it does not extend to an understanding of how to be happy and at peace. This can be seen in a number of areas such as how the vex plays, sleeps, eats, and cares for its young.

Vexes do not have the natural body fur that Noarfians possess, and this accounts for their need for cover at night, but it does not explain their desire for special sleeping costumes, their insistence on elaborate bedding, their inability to awaken during the night and play or work and immediately fall back to sleep, or their generally sour or distracted mood in the morning.

Although they do play, vexes could hardly be called playful. Their play must be scheduled rather than spontaneous, it always seems to contain devious attempts to injure or defeat their playmates, and if the play has not proven a vex superior, that vex can remain ill-tempered or depressed for hours or even days.

More curious still are their eating habits. A vex will not eat the same food over and over as will a Noarfian, thus requiring their masters to spend considerable time in food preparation. They will eat to the point that they gain weight or refuse to eat to the point that they begin to starve. They actually seem to prefer those foods that will adversely affect their bodies and those liquids that incapacitate their minds.

But perhaps strangest of all is the vexes' attitude toward their offspring. First, they appear to copy each other as to the number of offspring they will have. And once a baby vex is born, they become very confused as to how to care for it, the parents fight with each other even more than usual, and the routine they finally settle into is usually, once again, copied from what other vexes are doing at that time. As the baby vex grows older, the parents will often turn against it in subtle ways if it is not as large, intelligent, or attractive as other vexes its age. The average vex is so irritated with its offspring most of the time that it is a great puzzle as to why they have them at all.

When questioned about these and other unfortunate traits of the vex, Noarfians rush to their defense with one central argument: "They are powerful teachers of patience." And Noarfians indeed value vexes for the opportunities in forbearance and forgiveness they continually provide. In fact, the ancient folklore of the planet states that so prized has this lesson of patience always been, that a colony of Noarfians once took their vexes and settled a new planet called Earth, and then, in order to further enhance the power of the lesson, genetically arranged for the vexes to be the masters and for themselves to be the pets.

The Port of Timnor

The Rootcomb

The beings on the various inhabited planets are, as would be expected, at different levels of learning. Once a planet reaches completeness, it appears to vanish, even though it is actually more powerful than before. One planet close to this state is Timnor (from "time no more"). It is, except for one commercial port, composed mostly of unprojected thought. At this stage it can still be seen, but only as a translucent luminosity, like glass in water. The port itself is visually normal and resembles an industrialized island within a sea of soft light.

Even though all thought eventually takes form in the outer experience of the thinker, it does not take the form in which it is first seen within the mind. However, it can be made to do so, and manufacturing various types of thought-projectors is the industry of Timnor.

Most of the great explorers of the cosmos have been salesmen looking for new markets. Two such salesmen, in the latter parts of the sixth century B.C. and the nineteenth century A.D., presented a device made in Timnor known as a Rootcomb to the mystical teachers of Earth. This same device was also offered to Earth's sister planet, Terra, located in Lesser Halceon (a galaxy partially obscured by the Eta Carnia Nebula). These two planets have been thought of as sisters because their size, composition, age, and atmosphere are almost identical, and until the Rootcomb was accepted on Terra, the history of their life forms was also similar.

The Rootcomb, like all devices manufactured in Timnor, projects only thoughts of a carefully defined type. Any one device will not project *all* thought, for this would be so embarrassing that it could cause death. The Rootcomb was strictly designed for parents, and possibly it was because most of the Earth's spiritual leaders were not what could be called "devoted family men" that they rejected it.

The Rootcomb allows parents to see a future scene that will result from a present attitude. It cannot picture the results of an *action*, because, potentially, any action can be accompanied by a variety of divergent attitudes. (For example, getting a young child ready for school can be a time of humor and joining or a time of rush and irritation.) If a father who was in the habit of physically intimidating his son were to use the Rootcomb, he might dial in a future scene in which his son is intimidating a smaller child at school, and then a scene in which his son is intimidating his smaller partner in marriage, and then a scene in which he himself, now old and feeble, is being intimidated by his son. Obviously, such an exercise would have a profound effect on any caring parent, as it already has had upon millions on Terra. As it slowly became clear that there is no "limited attack" and that one individual's attitude can affect generations, Terra began to see itself as a single home and not as a holding pen for separate warring factions.

However, no matter how often it is offered, there may never be any wide acceptance of the Rootcomb by the inhabitants of Earth, mainly because of their deeply held ideal that one should rely on oneself and not on external means. This need not be a hindrance, though, because the one fact that salesmen from Timnor will not mention is that the Rootcomb, like any other object, is mere projected thought. The ability itself is inherent in the mind. Once one has the desire to see the true consequences of his attitudes, all he need do is close his eyes and he will see. When this insight has spread across the universe, Timnor will no longer need to manufacture thought-projectors, and its one visible port will vanish.

Fight hesitantly.
Judge halfheartedly.
Be happy unnecessarily.

PLANET: Guttorg

TRANSLATION: When the Intergalactic Council
established a retirement planet for professional
wrestlers, no one would have guessed that it would
quickly evolve into one of the most harmoniously run
societies in the cosmos. It turns out that, without ever
meaning to be, professional wrestling is a crash course
in how *not* to approach life. Anyone who survives the
occupation is on the brink of wisdom.

MEANING: Be slow to acquire new problems. The means
of accomplishing this is summed up on Guttorg in this
way:
Say what is easily forgotten.
Do what is easily overlooked.
Think what is everlasting.

Ribb and Fusia

Unlike humans, the people of Sai-nohp mate for life.
They don't marry, they simply form a deep friendship
and never abandon it. However, there was a period in
their recent history when this practice was brought into
question by Ribb and Fusia, a couple who ran a bed-
and-breakfast near one of the more conveniently located
spaceports.

Many of the couple's guests came from planets where
monogamy was a concept used mainly to inspire guilt in
one's departing partner. In talking to them over tea and
pufftillies (the traditional hairy tuber filled with steaming
peppers), Ribb and Fusia gradually became enthralled
with the almost limitless possibilities offered by divorce.
They saw that if you went about it intelligently, after
each divorce you could "trade up," gaining, over time,
ever more prosperous partners. You could accumulate
numerous children, stepchildren, and ex-stepchildren,
many bearing your name. As you grew older, you could
reexperience the bliss of finding dates, the importance of
falling in love, and, if you chose your new mates wisely,
have new and excessive sexual experiences with fresh,
young bodies (although you would, they were told, have
to put up with their "loud, stupid music"). Or, if you
chose, you could decide not to remarry at all and simply
avail yourself of other people's mates.

The problem was that on Sai-nohp divorce was unheard-of. No legal structure had ever been set up to process such a decision, and so when Ribb and Fusia held an open ceremony to formalize their experiment (first they had to marry, then divorce), their action attracted great interest, which, as the news traveled, eventually became planetwide. Their greatest exposure came when they appeared on the Bev Zattvorbytrxidrlij program.

Bev formatted their segment to include a panel composed of a sociologist, a psychologist, a manicurist, and several other behavioral authorities, all of whom had numerous questions for this modern couple on the cutting edge.

"Your concept of renouncing outmoded relationships is most interesting," said the sociologist, scooting forward in his chair. "I presume that as well as these 'singles' bars' you speak of, an advanced society would also have bars where families would go to trade their children."

"Now that you mention it," said Ribb, "that does seem natural, although none of our guests supplied us with any details."

"After you leave your life partner, are you supposed to remember his birthday?" asked the manicurist.

"No," said Fusia. "My understanding is that you're supposed to treat your ex like you'd never known him. Well, actually worse, because people are often nice to strangers."

" 'Ex'—an apt epithet," said the psychologist. "The symbol for a mistake. Something you erase."

"I don't think I could just ignore someone's birthday," said the manicurist. But Bev stepped in and moved things along by pointing out that ex-marrieds would lead to ex-children, ex-pets, ex-houses, etc., and wouldn't this be a spur to the economy.

"Yes," said the sociologist. "Each adult would require his or her own separate residence, houseplants, recliner, kitchen robot, et cetera. Thousands of lawyers specializing in divorce would be needed, new courts to handle these cases, new shows on holovision would be inspired—"

"Don't forget the new therapists that will be needed for the children," broke in the manicurist.

"To the contrary," said the psychologist. "Children are very resilient."

"And who knows, perhaps these children will share in the financial boom by writing best-selling books denouncing their parents and end up guests on this program!" said Bev. All but the manicurist seemed to agree that they should be so lucky.

However, none of these imagined benefits came to pass on Sai-nohp. It seemed that no one but Ribb and Fusia were willing to dare the risks of freedom. Finding no others who would cooperate, they eventually came back together, sold their bed-and-breakfast, and became makeup-color coordinators for Amway, which had just reached their solar system.

Laws of Attraction

The bodies of Peapwaudians are in the general shape of people throughout the cosmos—that is, what doesn't stick out, hangs down. And although their reproductive organs are located in their knees, the hearts and minds of young Peapwaudian lovers are equally influenced by the same law of sexual attraction that dominates most planets—namely, that desirability is based on scarcity. This is shown by the fact that for centuries elbows and noses have been covered (due, many paleontologists believe, to prehistoric attacks of the pointy-places mosquito), and as a result it is these parts of the body that two people of the opposite sex will first take note of (or, more accurately, take note of the *contours* of these parts, for they are always covered by the traditional nose and elbow bands). The knees themselves are not covered, and if asked why not, most Peapwaudians would probably laugh and point out the obvious need to have easy access to simple bodily functions, and besides, knees are not beautiful, lacking the sheer pointed grace of an elbow or a nose.

The larger the nose and the bonier the elbow, the more beautiful most Peapwaudians consider them to be, and possessing such obvious assets helps one to succeed not only in love but in business and anchoring the evening news. Comments frequently overheard, such as,

"Did you see those elbows?—how would you like to be married to her!" or, "Of course you're happily married, look at the size of your husband's nose!" indicate that, as on other planets, such considerations weigh heavily when selecting one's mate. However, as is universally true, making sound matrimonial choices is hampered by clothing.

The great controversy on the planet, media coverage of which sometimes preempts small wars, is over the growing tendency of magazines and museums to display these parts of the body openly in order to defend freedom of speech, and the increasing use among adolescents and other comedians of such expletives as "elbow grease!" and "wipe your nose!" and indecent phrases such as "rubbing elbows." Investigative reporters are presently spending a sizable percentage of their papers' budgets taking pictures of politicians looking at pictures. It is also quite common now to see calendars hanging in automotive repair shops and men's locker rooms of young women, shot from the elbows up, rubbing their bare noses.

No one knows where this will all end, but on older planets where the populations have grown weary of the entire subject, new parts of the body have had to be covered to restimulate the mating urge and revitalize the communications industry.

Dying is inconvenient, but don't let it ruin your life.

PLANET: Toxatron

TRANSLATION: This expression is one of many that were said to have been spoken to Oli Marmin, who, despite the best efforts of his friends, died of boredom and dust-mite allergies. Toxatron is a very exciting planet, but because of his fear of change, Oli was unable to perceive it that way. All he would do was stay in his cave room, doodling on the walls, making dust-ball castles on the floor, or lining up neat rows of rocks to throw at the next Stegosaurus look-alike that stuck its head in the door. Almost every day Oli's friends would drop by and say, "Oli, come out into the lighting. The volcanoes are erupting, the seas are boiling, it's a beautiful day!" But Oli was afraid to take risks.

MEANING: If you avoid all the big things, the little things will get you.

Oli Marmin looks askance

Milky Way Amusement Park

The true implications of many of the great sayings and parables go unrecognized on the planets where they originate. One of the most profound of these can be found on Earth, where the words, even though they have been set to rhyme and music and are not infrequently sung by large groups, have basically gone unheeded by the millions who have heard them. Not so, however, in other parts of the galaxy where "aliens," having listened to the words during their visits to Earth, have returned home to repeat them. As a result, they now hold the hallowed position of a galactic hymn.

The Milky Way Amusement Park, which occupies three planets and a moon, has constructed its main water ride around the theme of this hymn. Enlightenment Way, as it is called, is a thousand-mile-long river ride that could take as many years to complete. Yet, if traversed correctly, it can be completed easily within a day.

At the start of their journey, travelers are given only a copy of the hymn and a seat belt. At first they may not realize that the river moves deceptively fast, but this becomes increasingly evident the longer they are in their boats. Scattered along the river's path are alluring ports of pleasure whose sights and sounds promise countless means of easing one's way; mock wars on the shores over an endless list of issues on which one is enjoined to take sides; public service announcements on how turning around and rowing up the river would have cardiopulmonary benefits; signs that warn of indescribable disasters if one does not leave the river and portage over land; and spotlights of attention on other boats that have stopped to be outfitted in either fashionable or unconventional trimmings. Rapids, whirlpools, waterfalls, and bogs suddenly appear and disappear along the way. One is often sucked under or hurtled forward only to discover—if the disaster did not succeed in driving the traveler off the river—that the boat's progress has been unaffected and the journey's end is all the more assured.

The words of the hymn after which this ride is fashioned counsel that you must keep your hands busy in purposeful activity but that you must not take the activity too seriously, remembering always that the actual work is being carried on by the current of your destiny that conveys you upon its back. The hymn goes on to make this remarkable promise: that if you will but allow yourself to be carried along in this manner, you are guaranteed to be rewarded with four parts happiness to every three parts of noninterfering effort. Nor has the explanation been omitted for why this must be so, because the riddle of human life itself is solved in the hymn's final five words.

The actual wording of the hymn is very short and reads as follows: *Row, row, row your boat gently down the stream. Merrily, merrily, merrily, merrily, life is but a dream.*

Plants Are Their Own Reward

Before grass agreed to be walked on, before red roses agreed to share a vase with yellow ones, before evergreens agreed to grow out of holes cut in parking lots, before vegetables agreed to be cooked and eaten, and before trees agreed to be shredded for toilet paper, plants were rather balky. Seeing within fossils the evidence of plants' wilder days, interplanetary paleobotanists say, "Flora mellows as it gets older." However, it's not age that brings about the change so much as it is the dawning on plant consciousness that its day-to-day temperament could be improved. Take, for example, the planet Trebb Phillit Minor, which has been fairly typical in its botanical growth stages. When the Lamberattas (or Little People) first began making their homes among leaves and tendrils, plants on Trebb adopted a wait-and-see approach. But this did not last long.

As is true of most carbon-based bipeds, the Lamberattas began having wars as soon as they had broken into groups recognizable enough to know whom to fight. Although the first few skirmishes were fairly chaotic affairs, after several generations war became the primary social institution, with numerous laws and customs supporting it. The language itself grew to accommodate the many varieties of conflict. For example, wars waged by advanced nations on primitive peoples were called explo-

Flora mellows as it gets older

rations, expeditions, pacifications, or securing a happy campsite. Wars waged by strong nations on weak ones were called gifts of right government, steadying dominoes, or, in cases in which citizens themselves were the object of attack, restoring peace.

Soon, war in some form permeated all aspects of Lamberatta civilization: commercial wars, political wars, wars of words, wars of hemlines (because of their tendency to chap, most Lamberattas wear a loosely hanging garment similar to a smock). Special regulations were created for conflicts between parties of a marriage, between athletic teams, and between restaurants and customers who bite down on foreign objects in their soup. Laws were enacted about what one could and could not do to the neighbor's coddletrain (a loud six-legged reptile that can be taught to say "I love you"), and about what degree of carnage could be read, viewed, or acted out by different age groups for entertainment.

Before long (roughly two million years into Lamberatta evolution) the plants of Trebb had had enough. They were tired of their carpels being used as bunkers, their pistils as battering rams, their thorns as pikes, their reeds as blowguns, and their pollen sacs as chemical bombs. In short order, all hostile Lamberattas were thrown out of their leafy homes, ground cover refused to allow troop movements, and fruits and vegetables threw themselves up if eaten by combatants. The results were quick and dramatic. All war stopped on Trebb Phillit Minor.

Or so it first appeared. For although the Lamberattas were no longer overtly hostile, there was no real peace. War can be conducted on many levels, and the Lamberattas became masters at disguising attack. Stronger nations no longer plundered weaker ones, they simply manipulated them financially. Parents no longer spanked their children, they just beat them psychologically. The plants had changed the Lamberattas' behavior, but they had not changed their hearts.

And to the plants' surprise, war started among themselves. Gangs of young tomatoes began terrorizing preschool petunias and rolling over communities of retired horsetails. Bluestem would not allow prairie cordgrass to encroach upon their neighborhoods. And ivies began using their aerial roots to ensnare wind-borne seeds before they could even reach the ground. Consternation swept through the plant kingdom and no one could agree on what had happened or what to do about it.

In desperation the decision was made to awaken The Great Sequoia from its thousand-year sleep, and the first question the plants posed was why had fighting broken out among themselves.

In the crisp, balanced way that most trees have of talking, The Sequoia said:

You cannot both attack and love.
For if you look angrily at one thing,
you will look angrily at all things.
When you attack, you become an attacker.

"But how shall we deal with these exasperating Lamberattas?" asked the plants.

Slowly The Great Sequoia turned its wise, acerose, decurrent leaves toward the heavens. And then it spoke.

From this time on, be deeply yourself.
Your nature is to shelter, not be sheltered.
Your nature is to feed, not be fed.
Your nature is to give breath, not breathe.
Your nature is to delight, not be delighted.
Your nature is to love. And love is its own reward.

Yet the plants soon discovered that this was not an easy assignment. All they could do was set an example and hope that eventually it would be absorbed. But because doing this made them happier than forcing the mere empty forms of change on the Lamberattas, they continue to this day to be deeply themselves.

As for the Lamberattas, as might be expected, they missed the point entirely. Instead of studying themselves, they began intensive investigation of the plant kingdom, shocked into action by the plants' surprising revolt and precipitous return to passivity. Recently, scientists on Trebb have been puzzled by their latest discovery. When they amplified the tiny sounds ("squish," "crunch," "snap," etc.) that plants make when being eaten, they heard, not the "Ouch! Ouch! Ouch!" they had expected to hear, but the peculiar and troubling blessing, "You are what you eat."

Don't carve a glider out of the branch you're swinging from.

PLANET: Bambaroomp

TRANSLATION: One of three planets in the formation known as "The String of Pearls," Bambaroomp was once completely covered with a treelike growth in which the highly emotional Roomps lived and played. Oddly, their technological advances have been applied almost entirely to their toys—fighting kites, disks, flying pies, antigravitational boomerangs, poppums (heat-seeking paddles), and such, many of which are exquisitely sophisticated and daring. However, generations of war games and toy-lust have so decimated the vegetation and cluttered that which is left, that the planet is quickly becoming uninhabitable for arboreal beings.

MEANING: Don't misuse what sustains you. Those who pollute their minds with grievances and discontents will also pollute their bodies, their relationships, and their environment with equal disregard. Hence this corollary: **Littered minds create littered planets.**

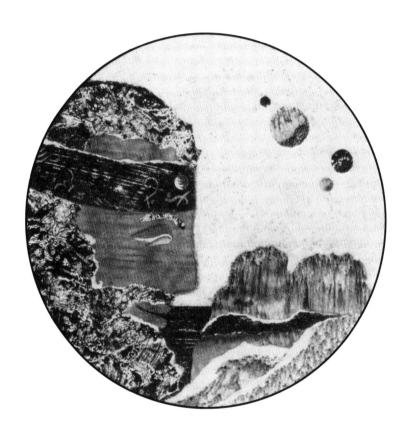

A portrait of Lazatar

Lazatar's Fire

On the sun side of Styn, in the cavetown of Issupulie,
lives a blacksmith whose forge is often encircled by
those who wait for him to pause in his work so that they
might ask a question, or by those who merely wait to
hear what answers Lazatar, the blacksmith, will give.

A long answer can take several hours to complete, for
when the color of the iron is right, it must be struck.
However, Lazatar is as great a speaker as he is a blacksmith and knows how to punctuate his answers with
grunts and bangs and long profound pauses in such a
way that his words are often drummed out as if spoken
from a thundercloud. Many a concluding sentence has
ended in a shower of sparks that has delighted his lis-
teners as noticeably as his wisdom has changed them.
The show is all the more dramatic because Lazatar is
blind.

One day a monk, who had traveled from the Isthmus
of Potii, asked Lazatar, "How does one dive from this
world to swim in the sea of God?"

"It is not so difficult," said Lazatar, flipping his mighty
mallet while he waited to see if the monk was there
merely to argue.

"Is it the reward for a life well spent?" the monk continued.

Satisfied that he was sincere, Lazatar said, "Death is

not the door to the heart of Life. God does not wait for a life to be spent before he bestows his peace."

"Can you tell us, then, what one must do?"

"Gladly," said Lazatar, but so long did he work after making this promise that the monk began to think that his answer was that one must become a blacksmith.

Suddenly Lazatar closed his bellows and said, "During the reign of the Empire of Equality, there was a man who, like you, strove to live his life immaculately. This one, whose name was Jameel, came into the world strongly sensitive to the waters of Reality, and after many years of faithfully performing the duties that the Empire divided to him, decided that his time to awaken had come. So Jameel sat on a stone by the ocean, looked out to sea, and began a single chant. His words were: 'You are everything I want. You are everything I need. You are everything I am. I drown in the ocean of Your love.'

"It was not long before the authorities discovered that Jameel was no longer doing his share of the country's work, and they promptly threw him into prison. Still he did not divert his eyes from the direction of the ocean or make any sounds but the sounds of his chant.

"When it was brought to the Warden's attention that, even though using very few words, Jameel was speaking more than his share, the Warden ordered that his tongue be removed.

"Now Jameel could only mouth his chant with his lips alone, but this he did with reverence, and he held his gaze toward the sea.

"Again the guards reported Jameel to the Warden: 'Although making no sound, he is still attempting to speak more than his share.'

" 'His intention is the same,' said the Warden. 'Not even the appearance of inequality will be tolerated.' And he ordered that Jameel's lips be removed.

"Thus was Jameel left with only the deep inner music of his chant and the outward focus of his eyes.

"But still the guards were not satisfied. This time they returned to the Warden and pointed out that during the period when all the prisoners were supposed to sleep, Jameel, by keeping his eyes opened toward the sea, was using more than his share of wakefulness. Naturally, the Warden had no choice but to order his eyes removed also.

"Now was Jameel left with no outward way of worshiping, and yet his heart did not cease to chant and his mind did not cease to focus on the ocean of God's love. And when the guards returned to Jameel's cell to see how else they could torture him, they found only a tongue, a pair of lips, and two eyes."

Lazatar picked up his bellows and turned toward the monk. "You asked what one must do in order to enter the sea of God. The answer is, there is nothing to do, because anything you set out to do can be thwarted. There is only something to decide. Do, therefore, whatever you must, but decide that God is the only thing you want. Decide this, and God will welcome you with a dance more joyous than the dance of fire welcoming air." And with these words Lazatar sent such a blast from his bellows onto the open furnace grate that many who were present say that for an instant all of Issupulie glowed with the light of Lazatar's fire.

Cathray Canute

The roar of the tyrannosaur is so loud that the children standing in line have to wear ear mufflers, and still there is sometimes a slight pain reported. Only one child at a time is allowed into the open-field cage, the height and weight limitation being no child over seven feet, two hundred pounds (because of the time it takes the tyrannosaur to swallow larger bodies). This is the most popular event in all the Cathray Parks, despite the fact that the tyrannosaur needs less than a minute to chase down even the speediest child. Most of them, however, are so weakened with laughter that the beast can do its job in a matter of seconds. Off-planet parents are advised not to watch because most of them find it disturbing to see the little kicking legs of their children disappear along with their muffled howls of laughter.

—ACCOUNTS OF CATHRAY CANUTE

On the planet of yibb-Ya-nozz, the ordinary laws of cause and effect do not apply. It formed seven billion years ago within the cusp of a barred-helix time shift, and the normal sequence of intention-process-outcome has been in free-form suspension (up for grabs) ever since. The best-seller *Accounts of Cathray Canute* is discounted as fiction in most galaxies, but the stories are actually candid observations by Neutsoy, Cathray's twin stepmother, who is a practiced and astute observer.

From the book, the reader learns that Cathray makes a comfortable living reconditioning dinosaurs for her Children's Parks. She picks only carnivorous ones with a natural gait, snatching them from the spiked tails and horns of vegetable eaters. She transports them live from the Mesozoic era and feeds them a high-priced tranquilizer. Then she caps their teeth in foam, infuses their systems with a genetically engineered, climate-control bacterium, gives them a neighborly, moderate-size, primate brain, and, by means of an eye tuck, adds the hint of a smile to their lipless mouths. By the time they wake up, they are not what you would call works of art, but when they chase down the children and swallow them live, they seem relatively happy with their new role.

A simple collapse in time restores the children to their predigested selves and they are left with only a few graphic photographs and a whopping big story to tell when they return home.

Cathray (as well as the parents who bring their children to the parks) is sometimes criticized for this apparently violent though physically harmless form of play. Often denounced along with those who allow children to play with war toys, Cathray has for many years conducted follow-up studies on the long-term effects of being eaten alive. None of the children, she claims, has yet to grow up to be masticatistic. "When one child says, 'Bang! Bang! You're dead,' and the other child falls down, only to rise up laughing a few seconds later, their perception of death is actually more accurate than that of the angry parent who grabs the toy gun and sends the child to its room."

But her critics answer that it's easy for Cathray to make these pronouncements from a planet where the effects of time can be erased by love and laughter. On ordinary planets, if adults don't teach children to stop having fun playing war, with just what kind of attitude are they going to grow up?

Don't look a horse in the mouth when you're riding it.

PLANET: New Wapavapu

TRANSLATION: Although the primary animal used for transportation on New Wapavapu is not called a horse, it does whinny and swat flies with its tail. However, it can grow to be five meters tall and must be mounted by means of its long, knotted mane.

MEANING: Those who look down on their abilities, fall down. On this planet of many gifted people, it has become a value, especially among the younger generation, to turn against any livelihood that comes easily, especially if it does not give the appearance of a "higher calling." Since this form of self-deprecation is considered mere arrogance, the above maxim is sometimes linked with another ancient saying: **Righteousness hardens the arteries. The way to remain flexible is to stay confused.**

Mijirimi and his son

The Power That
Brings Happiness

When Traj reached nine, the age of right and wrong, he came to Sa Mijirimi with a question. "Father, it is said that on all of Vaesulka you are the greatest magician, and if you are not, I know that at least there is none greater, since you can do anything."

When Mijirimi started to object, his son held up his hand and said, "Father, I am not here to argue this point. I am here to ask you why do you not put your powers to better use?"

"I am sorry you find fault with one who can do anything," said Mijirimi, smiling. "But tell me, my only son, what better use is there than to delight people and make them happy?"

"Your audiences may leave The Great Dome entertained," said Traj, "but very often the lives they must return to are not happy. If you wished, you could give them all in life that they seek."

"This question is perhaps even more serious than you realize, so rather than give you mere words, let us witness the answer together."

Mijirimi took his son to the market town of Ot, where they stood for a while watching the lines of shoppers move slowly past the many open-air stores. "A life is made up of moments. If each moment can be made happy, the entire life is happy. Here before you is the time of buying and selling, a moment that is common to all people's lives. Tell me, who among these shoppers do you wish to have the life that is being sought?''

Traj did not hesitate but picked out an elderly woman who was having difficulty maneuvering among those younger and more aggressive than she.

First, Mijirimi gave her increased physical strength, which the woman seemed to sense, for she began standing her ground when other buyers tried to nudge her aside. As her confidence continued to grow, she herself started moving aside buyers who were in her way.

Then Traj realized that something else was occurring. Just as the woman would step before a display of produce, the vendor would begin setting out the fresher fruits or vegetables he had been holding in reserve, and reducing the price of the older produce, even though it was not the end of the market day. Thus the woman always got her pick of the best of both.

Drawing Traj aside, Mijirimi said, ''What do you notice so far, my son, about my influencing events to make life turn out the way one person wishes?''

''If the woman is first, other shoppers are not. If the woman saves money, the vendors lose. The conclusion is obvious: power cannot favor one person without slighting another.''

''And what of the woman herself? Do you sense that she is happier?''

Traj watched the woman a moment longer and said, ''No, she seems harder and more aggressive, and anxious that her luck will run out. I cannot say she is happier. However, this is a marketplace, and these are the dealings of strangers. Within a friendship, within a marriage, within a family, where the interactions are based on intimacy, certainly you could arrange for one to have the life that is sought.''

Mijirimi returned all circumstances in the marketplace to the way they were before and then walked with his son a little farther until they came within sight of a small store filled with fine, well-proportioned pottery. Mijirimi stopped and said, "There you see a husband and wife who have talent as artists and skill as merchandisers. Near them, playing behind that small stone barrier, are their two children. Unlike many couples, they are fair with each other and divide all duties. However, it cannot be said they have all in life that they seek, even at this very moment. Choose, therefore, one of them to receive all."

"I suspect," said Traj, "that being artists each of them would rather be doing something more creative than simply minding the store or tending children, but surely the wants of the littlest child are few and he could be given the life he seeks."

Mijirimi nodded and instantly the child crawled over the barrier to a display of bowls and began pulling them onto the floor. Soon they were broken, and his parents, instead of interfering, joined him and began tossing the pieces into the air, while the older sibling sat quietly aside, strangely dazed and contented.

"Within this moment," said Mijirimi, "the child, receiving what he wants most, which is the full attention of both his parents, is indeed happy, but how long will he remain so after the family business fails, the creative needs of his parents go unfulfilled, and his older sibling wakens from his stupor and becomes jealous and resentful?" Having said this, Mijirimi returned the family and its store to the way it was before.

"I see," said Traj sadly. "The powers you possess cannot make life work. They are of little significance."

"You have seen correctly that the power I have to control events is of little meaning. The only power worth having, everyone already has. It lies not in bending others to your will, but in the willingness to pass over one's own discontents like water passes over the stones of a riverbed. If water refused to proceed until all impediments were removed, it could not do its mighty work of purifying itself and nourishing the living. The power that brings happiness, my son, is the power of absolute gentleness, not the power of absolute control."

The Invisible Teacher

The tradition within many of the nations on Muggarue is for one to place oneself under the tutelage of a spiritual Guide or "Escort," and there is often great pride taken in this relationship. Those few who hold the position of Escort are by far the most noticeable inhabitants. They often wear lighted capes and exquisite spinning headpieces and smoke the Royal Jalupa, a fluted reed that emits both music and fragrance.

There is, however, one Escort few people wish to acknowledge as their own, but who nevertheless follows relentlessly those she has decided are ready to learn. She is known within her meager following as the "Invisible Teacher" (IT), because, although she can be heard plainly, she cannot be seen, and hence no pride can be taken in having her as one's Escort. In fact, most people consider her followers self-deceived as to her very existence. Unlike other Escorts who claim for their various teachings the end to all worldly problems, IT refuses to give practical advice. Instead, she makes arbitrary statements such as, "Bliss cannot be translated into a usable skill," and, "If it can be proven within the world, it has no validity."

Perhaps the core of IT's teaching is that "beneath the garments of the world is Joy." "The mind," she teaches, "dresses everything it sees in costumes. Strip these away and you will see the Face of Merriment."

There was once a philosopher who was much re-
spected for his championing of humanitarian causes in
books and articles published throughout the planet. On
the advice of a friend, he came to a small meeting of
IT's followers and asked if their Escort could save his
marriage. Before they could answer, IT's voice gently
filled the minds of all who were present.

"I cannot guarantee you even one more day with your
spouse, but I can easily place in your hand the key to
your heart if not to hers: Whenever you come before
her, take off your worldly identity and become the companion that she needs."

"But does this mean," asked the philosopher, "that I
must renounce my work?"

"Certainly not. Continue doing what you do and do it
well, but never deceive yourself that it is 'your work.' It
is easy to see the goodness in large groups with which
one has little contact. Only a small effort is needed to
love the poor, a former enemy state, those who have a
certain illness, a disadvantaged nation, or a neglected
minority. But enormous effort is required to accept and
commit to the perfect seed of innocence that is within
the ordinary people who surround you. Yet it is this effort that transforms the spirit and unifies the mind."

Although the philosopher left and never returned to
the IT meetings, one can now detect within his writings
a strange absence of outrage.

What you haven't done does not exist.

PLANET: Willawai

TRANSLATION: Everything that Snos touched became neat. He was so exceptionally clean and well organized that even the thought of something left undone was intolerable. And yet there were still many things for Snos to do. On Willawai, as on all other planets, there is no Higher Order or Natural Limit placed on what needs to be done. "There's no end to it" is truly a cosmic complaint. In one way, however, Snos was lucky. He had a mother who still told him what to do. Of course, that alone was not his luck; his luck was that he listened. After he had received the National Tidy-up Award for the third straight year, Snos's mother phoned him. "Snos," she said, "are you happy?" "No, Mother," he said. "Despite what other people think, I don't ever seem to get on top of things." "Snos," she said, "how many things do you have left to do?" He pulled out his newly revised list. "Two hundred and fifty-six." "Snos," she said, "if you work very hard, if you devote the rest of your life to getting everything done, when you die you *may* have only two hundred forty-six things left." "Oh," said Snos. "Did you know," lied his mother, "that two hundred forty-six is only twelve fewer than the national average?" "I didn't know that," said Snos.

"Trust me," said his mother. "Now, Snos, is twelve fewer what you want to live your life for?" Being a wise mother, she already knew what the answer would be.

MEANING: The key to happiness is to focus on what exists.

Marks of the Master

Xrrota "Xota" T'ro is known throughout the inner quadrant of the Andromeda Galaxy as "the ultimate master" because of her willingness to go to any extreme to induce enlightenment. Many of her disciples at the Shrine of Sildivia have dents and bruises, and a few even missing fingers, from the blows she administers to emphasize her points. All of this she manages to do not only without anger but with noticeable affection. Consequently, these "marks of the master" are worn with honor by her disciples.

A merchant who was shopping for a master decided to test Xota with a chronic problem. He complained to her that he lost his inner quiet whenever his wealthiest customer tried to talk him into lowering his prices.

"Some of your poorer customers also try to bargain with you, but this does not disturb you. Am I correct?" asked Xota.

"Yes," conceded the merchant.

"Therefore, it is not the rich man's bargaining that upsets you; it is the fact that although you have wealth, it is less than his."

"Perhaps this is true," replied the merchant, "but what can I do?"

"If you begrudge a rich man his wealth, give him everything you have. Then there will be nothing to compare."

Tain'say seeks Counsel from Xota

The merchant departed, knowing that he was not ready for Xota.

All who study at the Shrine of Sildivia do so voluntarily; nevertheless, objections to Xota's methods are frequently heard. Once, after removing a disciple's finger, she answered his outcry with, "Why do you worry? You will get several new ones in your next life, unless, that is, you are ready to awaken from all lives now." On the occasion when she lopped off an ear, she said, "You have had a thousand different ears and what good use have you ever put them to? Maybe now at least one ear will begin to hear." At another time she pulled a hair from the heads of four disciples who had been brought to her for falling asleep while meditating. Into each disciple's hand she dropped a hair from one of the others' heads. Then she said, "The body, which can withdraw into sickness, sleep, and death, is merely your notion that you can separate from God. And now you think that a strand of your hair is separate from you. Yet where did the hair fall but into the hand of your brother? And where can you fall but into the hand of God?"

The Shrine of Sildivia resembles more a small community than the traditional Andromeda shrine. This is because Xota encourages all her disciples to marry, have children, and, except when receiving instruction, to live as normal a life as possible, including pursuing a trade. One day, Tain'say, a beloved disciple, came to her and said, "Master, working all day as a stone cutter I come home tired, and after I have fed the children and played with them awhile, the time comes to put them to sleep. It is at this point that my recognition of unity begins to vanish, because all I can think of is getting to sleep myself. Any delay—and with five children there are many— turns my heart against them."

"Tain'say, your goal is not to play with the children," answered Xota. "Your goal is to be one with them. Playing with them is merely the context. Your goal is not to feed the children. Your goal is to be one with them. Feeding them is merely the context. Likewise, your goal is not to put the children to sleep. Your goal is to be one with them. Putting them to sleep is merely the context."

"Master, you have taught me this thought and I have repeated it to myself many times, and when I feed them and play with them I follow it. It is only when the time for them to sleep comes that I fail."

"You can experience inner harmony only when your mind is at one with what you are doing. If your goal is for another time, you will know distress. When you feed them, you feed them. When you play with them, you play with them. But when you put them to sleep, you do so in order that *you* may sleep, therefore your mind is split and fights itself."

"But by that time I am too tired to concentrate."

"Tiredness is not the problem. It requires no more alertness to do a task for its own sake than to do it for another. If you knew that your time to die would come upon completing the task of putting your children to sleep, you would have no difficulty using these moments to join with them rather than to separate."

"Yes, I can see that this would be true, but I also know that I will not die."

"Then I will help you. Tonight, if you do not use this time to join with your children, I promise to kill you."

"This would indeed solve the problem," said Tain'say, "but you would never do that."

Xota giggled. "That is exactly what you said last life."

(That evening, while putting his children to bed, Tain'say received enlightenment.)

Phizz

The curve of space that forms each island universe creates an original shape. When seen from without, the fifth universe (where the Milky Way is found) has a distinctive bulge like a camel's hump. On the outer rim of this semiovoid lie three galaxies in which the original inhabitants of the life-bearing planets are "spawned," that is, born at the same time. However, once they begin reproducing, age differences among their offspring result and these increase with each generation. Eventually, every planet achieves a full range of ages.

On the newer planets, the first generation or two is greatly prized by inhabitants of the older planets, and travel agencies offer special vacations to the planet that has the age group of one's choice. Only those worlds inhabited entirely by infants are considered too dangerous to visit.

Although not the most popular, unquestionably the most challenging is Phizz, the planet of teenagers. When surveyed, travel agencies list four main categories of customers who book stays there. Members of the first category expect the visit to be a way of recapturing their youth. Tourists citing this reason are seldom repeat customers.

The motives of the second group are harder to classify, but the lure of sheer oddity seems the attraction.

When questioned, they say things like, "I love wildlife parks and I'm told this is a step up"; or, "My therapist says I need to go someplace where I'll be totally ignored"; or, "I'm hard-of-hearing and I've been told I'll have no trouble on Phizz."

The third group is composed of professionals (rock stars, jeans designers, religious missionaries). The Church of Conscientiousness, for example, sends missionaries regularly, even though they have always had great difficulty communicating the church's central message—that cleanliness is next to godliness. The missionaries are instructed to begin by teaching the inhabitants basic spiritual practices such as putting the cap back on the toothpaste, taking out the trash, and not throwing underwear on the floor. Should this ever succeed, they are then to teach clean language and clean thought. Missionaries returning from Phizz with any discernible residue of goodwill are considered candidates for priesthood.

A strange compulsiveness is inherent in the fourth group—lecturers who persistently demand that they be booked on Phizz, despite the prospect of low fees, sullen audiences, frequent interruptions, and no applause. Evidently the urge to lecture teenagers is so universal that many geneticists now believe it is hereditary.

Some visitors do not fall into any category, and perhaps the most famous of these is Tollallee, from the oracle planet of S'in D'asph. Her love of Phizz is renowned, and when questioned why she visits it so often, she answers, "To witness dayspring." Adolescence, she teaches, is the most concentrated of all growth stages. "The lessons of an entire life are reviewed, but reviewed so quickly that many visitors miss the significance of what they are seeing. As the largest trees disguise their destinies in the smallest seeds, so do adolescents disguise the buddings of wisdom."

When others object to this viewpoint, as they usually do, Tollallee may add one final explanation: "If one cannot see the first green shoots of wisdom, at least no one should fail to see that teenagers possess the eight attributes of right living: They are willing to question authority and self-evident truths. They are willing to explore unthought-of paths. They are willing to stare into danger's eye. They are willing to bring immense energy to what they do. They are willing to believe there is a way. They are willing to close all doors but the present. They are willing to fire their souls with an ideal. And most significantly, they are willing to have fun. Seek, therefore, to cast no shadow over teenagers' efforts or motives. In all probability, the child still burns more brightly in them than in you."

A family of smuths

Better to stoop with the weight of a smuth than to chase after quantumberries.

PLANET: Ixili

TRANSLATION: A smuth, the sacred animal of Ixili, is a soft edgeless mammal and the only life-form on the planet that has fur. Unless caught by an anticruelty society, it can live for up to three hundred years and is usually passed down from one generation to another within a family. Many claim that smuths are telepathic because their primary animal sound, a quiet good-natured chuckle, seems to occur only when the person holding one begins to worry. However, some zoologists say that they are merely sensing minute muscular tensions and instinctively defending their territory. Although smuths usually sleep on people's laps, the above saying refers to their habit of jumping onto the back (and instantly going to sleep) of anyone who leans over for more than a few seconds to do a task. Even though it is awkward to remain in this position, it is considered improper to disturb the rest of the sacred animal of Ixili.

MEANING: Money is not happiness, respect, love, power, or excitement. Money is simply money. Within Ixili's monetary system, quantumberries are the highest denomination and to "chase after" them means to be possessed by a desire for something that has no heart.

Putting It in There

In Bladd, the wealthiest of the principalities on Flagan-Illip, many individuals believe that their favorable circumstances result from the practice of "putting it in there." If a new hovermobile, a new job, a new child, a new garglelot (a previously owned lover) is desired, when one "puts it in there," the Ethereal Code is activated and one receives what is wanted.

Working in Bladd is a short, stocky émigré from one of the poorer, war-torn principalities, a prominent theophysicist known affectionately as Aunt Brass, a name she acquired because of her passionate personality and tuba-like voice. When first visiting Bladd she became interested in discovering what was the "it" that was "put in there," since she could find no article on the subject in any scientific journal. Finally, she learned from a man she cornered in a Food for Precognitions store that "it" was a statue, widely available in stores such as his. Whenever one had a specific wish, this statue, representing the Short-Order Angel, must be placed in the Short-Order Shrine, kept in one's meditation room. Nothing more was required.

After conducting numerous studies, none of which, despite her prominence, she was able to get published, Aunt Brass put out a small pamphlet containing her findings entitled *In Every Life a Little Sunshine Must Fall.* She had taken the four most-asked-for items—parking places, bargains, a more spiritual job, and a new mate—and instructed the first test group to "put it in there" in the usual manner, the second test group to pursue these four categories through goal setting and planning, and the control group to simply keep careful records of how often they received what they wanted without thought or effort. The first group was successful 18 percent of the time, the second group, 19 percent, and the control, 17 percent.

It was not long before several assemblies of higher learning had replicated her work, and a professor from one of these called on Aunt Brass to discuss a new theory. His assumption was that the fault with the old method of PIT (putting it in there) was the use of an external, nonmental facilitator, namely the statue.

"Is it not true that you postulate a Shared Nucleus within all minds, and conclude that the observable universe is a construct of this joint mental essence?"

"Precisely!" boomed Aunt Brass.

"In that case, PIT should be performed within the mind. Instead of putting a statue into a shrine, one should put one clear thought into consciousness. In other words, if one held in the mind a single idea of what one wanted, the Shared Nucleus would manifest it in the externalized world."

"It isn't that *nothing* would come of this, but the results, my good professor, would be equally inconsistent," said Aunt Brass, waggling her finger. "Think of all the people who must be controlled and all the events that must be altered for one to obtain—with absolute consistency—a mere parking place near the entrance of every popular establishment that one frequents. Now think of the millions of children born with physical defects and disease, some with only moments to live. In each of these cases there is only one innocent, unborn child to control. And during the long period that each of those mothers carries her child within her, does she not hold in thought, does she not focus, does she not will, does she not *pray* for a healthy child? And what of the millions of fathers who are, right now, watching their young sons starve to death? Are they not holding in thought one thing and one thing only: food for their child? And in these instances, as with a thousand others I could cite, there is not even any selfishness in the desire."

"Of what use, then, is your theory?" asked the professor. "What good does it do us to know that there is a common core of consciousness running through all our minds if we cannot use it?"

"We cannot use it, but we can be it. And if we were to be it, there would no longer exist a desire to use anyone or to seek an advantage over any living being. To do so would merely be to divide ourselves. In other words, if we were to be it rather than use it, we would know love."

It was with some sadness that the professor had to return to his colleagues and report that Aunt Brass was as unscientific as her name.

The Salesman

A passage from one of the holy scriptures of the planet Zigtara reads: *If the mind of the child has one honest thought, truth will take root in the heart. If the eye of the child has a single tear, that tear will become a river that will float the child back to the heart of the Divine. Therefore, do not despair for anyone.*

A salesman who once lived on Zigtara went from door to door selling computerized holy men for home inspiration. He was not sincere. But he knew a good product when he saw one. Gradually he learned when to say "Praise A!" and when to say "Praise B!" Gradually he learned what passages from the various scriptures to call up on his wristband monitor. Sometimes he encountered people who were truly devout and he had to speak words that would be of interest to them. What he didn't realize was that these words contained true goodness that echoed within the forgotten goodness of his heart. The more he spoke the words of truth, the more conscious he became of the truth within him. In the end, he did not attain devoutness itself, but he did become harmless. And on the planet of Zigtara, where arguments are concluded by exchanging bites, this is a substantial accomplishment.

Beloved, God heard you the first time.

PLANET: Leconk

TRANSLATION: Because Leconk experiences an almost
continuous shower of meteorites, prayers are of
necessity short.

MEANING: Do not be afraid. All your questions have
been anticipated. On planets where the life span is
considerably longer than on Leconk, the notion that
God speaks in vague signs and coded indicators, that
the meaning of events must be painstakingly raked
over, or that one must keep calling in one's request to
The Head Switchboard indefinitely, have evolved out
of an excess of time. While on Leconk, where there is
not enough time to second-guess, it is assumed that
the answer is in your heart before you ask.

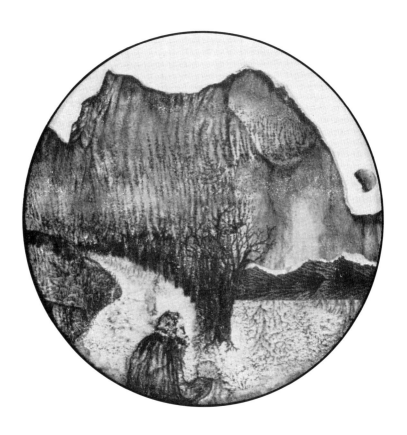

Torzol without his sword

The Legend of Oneness

In feverish dreams Torzol still could feel himself meld with the steel of his sword as it plunged through the heart of his enemy. Not that he was a killer. He had never killed in anger, never struck a blow at the weak or the young. He killed from pure righteousness, from clarity of vision. And throughout the planet Kalpretni he had been honored mightily for his strength of purpose and immaculate execution. How he had loved that word, *execution.*

He could not remember the first doubt, the first question. His conscious mind had dismissed it, but it had taken root in unconscious thought, where it had festered and grown into the monstrosity that had destroyed his power and stilled his sword. Now Torzol knew only doubt.

A warrior cannot see the heart of his enemy, cannot share his pain or recognize his goals. A warrior cannot walk into the shadow of understanding and remain whole. But the words of a dying man had betrayed him, only one man of many whose last moments were spent staring at the glitter of his steel. At the time, the words had merely puzzled him: "My brother, I weep for you." He had looked again at the man as death seized him. He was no brother, only one who stood in the way of righteousness. And then he had laughed at the man's stupidity.

Torzol remained frozen in doubt for eight years. What right had a dead man to weep for *him*, the unconquerable Torzol, the slayer of thousands? And how could a man he had seen only for an instant know him sufficiently to weep?

Kalpretni was not a planet that tolerated questions, that admitted uncertainty. And his betrayal of righteousness did not go unnoticed as it ate into his soul, as it collected around his body until he was flabby and weak with dissipation. No one followed him now, for he did not know where he was going. What reward could he promise anyone? Shared grief, shared misery? Guilt had never touched him before but now its torture pierced every waking and sleeping moment. He had allowed himself to become weak. He had allowed himself to doubt. Surely death was the only answer—to join these so-called brothers in defeat.

For the last time Torzol unsheathed his sword, and in the light of his fire he sharpened it until, once again, it shone with the brilliance of righteousness. He strode into the barren winter trees that surrounded his encampment and made his way to the small clearing where he often wandered in torment to stand for a moment gazing at the black skies, or to look over the valley at the continually burning fires of torched villages. Here would he end his uncertainty.

Torzol did not tremble at the deed he was to undertake. He would draw his sword into him with such force that it would pierce him through, and even if he did not die immediately, he would quickly bleed to death or more probably be torn apart by the wild dogs that roamed these hills. The thought pleased him.

He stood in the moonlight and faced the final thrust. The point of the sword against his heart was all he could see. He would now die in the purity of its cold superiority. But then he felt them gathering around him, felt their presence, those he had killed, and the "brother" who had planted the seed of his destruction. Had they come to claim his soul in retribution? They gave off a curious glow that dulled the light of his sword. One of them stepped forward, and although he could not see anything but softly lit shadow, he knew who this was. And finally Torzol trembled.

"Torzol, your time of consummation approaches. You have seen oneness and yet you have continued to deny it. Leave now your sword in the bowels of the earth and go forth to teach oneness to your brothers. Renunciation of your destiny is all that has been tormenting you these long years."

"I cannot. I no longer wish to live with disgrace as my companion. I no longer want to feed the cancer of my doubt."

"Bury your sword now and know that divine doubt has washed you clean. Go forth and teach the oneness of mankind."

"I do not know how to teach this oneness. I do not know what it looks like. What of the enemy, what of those who are evil, what of those who would take my life? Surely you are not asking me to include them in oneness."

"Indeed, this is what I am asking."

"They will attack me and I will die."

"Had you not intended to die?"

"Yes, but die with honor."

"Torzol, there is no honor in repeating the same mistakes that have been passed through history in tedious refrain. There is no honor in refusing to live when you have no life. There is honor in living what you see. I do not tell you that to do so will shield you from pain, or even death, but I do tell you that if you must die, at least you will die with vision, and that is not real death."

"I do not understand. I cannot teach."

"You answered the call the day you slew me on the battlefield."

"I answered no call."

"From that moment on you could no longer strike your brother. Indeed you answered." And with those words the victims of his past left Torzol alone with his sword.

That night Torzol dug a mighty pit and, climbing down into it, laid his sword at the bottom. Having filled it with dirt and stones, he pulled up eight trees, one for each year of his exile, and he stacked them like a spire over the mound. Aside from this one act, Torzol's behavior changed only slightly in the days that followed. He did not go forth to harangue crowds in what was left of the village squares. And with those he encountered on the roads he walked, he did not argue, he did not thwart, he did not oppose. He merely fed the wild dogs of the hills, carried water to the shrubs near his camp, extinguished the fires that threatened his grasslands and forest, and gave shelter to the few who fled battle.

Then the day came when Torzol knew that he must now meet the gaze of fear with the gaze of love. Leaving behind what little he possessed, he walked for many days until he came to the encampments of his enemy. At first, because this was Torzol and because of the suspicious fact that they could see no weapon upon him, the warriors he approached stepped aside and would not confront him. But at last one man stood his ground and said, "If you have a weapon, draw it now, or else you will die."

"I have no weapon," said Torzol, "for I am not your enemy."

"Of course you are my enemy," answered the warrior. "You come from the direction of my enemy, you wear the clothes of my enemy, you bear the name of my enemy."

Torzol opened the breast of his tunic and said, "Look, my brother. I am flesh of your flesh, blood of your blood. Only in one's thoughts can one be an enemy, and I hold no wish that you be harmed."

The warrior began to doubt and slowly lowered his sword, but as he did, those who had gathered around started yelling for him to put up his guard, that this was a trick. Suddenly the warrior stepped forward and drove his sword through Torzol's heart and withdrew the blade in a single motion.

As the warrior bent over the bleeding body of his enemy to search for the concealed weapon that he knew must be there, he heard Torzol whisper, "My brother, I weep for you."

When no weapon could be found on Torzol, word went forth confirming what for many years had been suspected—that in the last years of his life, Kalpretni's great warrior had become demented and had lost his courage and his will. Only his attacker doubted in his heart that this was so.

Death is a window but life is a door.

PLANET: Serin

TRANSLATION: Perhaps the most poetic of all planets is Serin, where the population speaks in meter and often in rhyme. Poetry is traditionally associated with idyllic conditions, but because the land is poor and the climate harsh, life on Serin is difficult. The planet's historians believe that the verselike quality of the language was born of working songs and the chants needed to coordinate mass hard labor, which on Serin seems endless. When Serinans were recently given the opportunity to move to a newly discovered planet that was far more hospitable than their own, many observers were surprised that, even after most of them had visited it, only one small township elected to move. Interviewed as to why she had not wanted to leave, one Serinan was quoted as saying:

> We've learned to take the troubles we face
> As means of giving and gaining embrace.
> If we move to a place that fits like a glove,
> We'll just have to search for a reason to love.

MEANING: Rest offers a glimpse of liberty. Life offers the choice to be free.

Masti the Mormikon

In most lives a time is reached when one can see the patterns of one's past. Illusions are dropped, at least temporarily, and the world is honestly appraised. On most other planets, this moment is termed a crisis point because many react to what they have seen by judging their life harshly and turning against any who are a part of it. In only one small section of the cosmos is this reaction sometimes precluded.

The comet Borzorgia is the only known heavenly body that travels across multiple galaxies. It circles the central star cluster of the sixth universe, and its billion-light-year orbit pierces eleven galaxies before it completes its circuit. It affects any inhabited planet that it passes near, and Masti the Mormikon has made it his life work to follow in its wake to help the victims of Borzorgia's mysterious gravitational pull.

The comet primarily affects those who are having midlife crises. An honest appraisal of their lot can cause individuals to step back in disgust, and this response is sometimes so deep that they may find themselves outside their bodies, looking down on the remains of their youthful dreams. As Borzorgia passes near an inhabited planet, those few who find themselves so displaced are sucked up by the comet's gravitational pull and cast into the outer layers of the planet's noosphere. The victims usually believe that their lives have ended and that they are now lost in some kind of purgatory, when in fact their bodies, although temporarily dazed, remain very much alive.

While they are in this state, Masti the Mormikon pays his visit. Having the aerial abilities that all Mormikons possess, he floats up to each one and asks, "Do you have any regrets?" Naturally, their greatest regret is that they are dead, but thinking that this is an advance man from the other side, they begin reviewing their lives and the legacies they have left behind from a broader perspective. Many of them see for the first time the effects they had on the hundreds of lives they encountered.

"Is that how you had intended to live your life?" asks Masti. If their hearts cry out, "No!" Masti will then say, "You may return to your body, but remember, there are more profound things to lose than life."

"But how will I remember once I return?" they ask. And Masti's answer is always the same: "I have placed in your heart a vessel of light. Every time you remember to make another's happiness your own, the vessel will spill forth its contents and peace will flow through you. Yet, when you forget, the light will return to its vessel, patiently to await your future welcome."

The deed that Masti performs in the wake of Borzorgia is only a more specialized application of the service given by all Mormikons throughout the cosmos. Elsewhere, when the mind is asleep and silent between dreams, a Mormikon approaches the spirit as it hovers just above the body. It places its vessel within the heart and gently whispers this message: "You have already lost greater opportunities than the opportunity to awaken and live for one more day. Go forth *this* day and lose no more." It is because this message is occasionally accepted that even people with hopeless lives will sometimes awaken quite happy.

Skipping Child

It is reported, not as historical fact but as legend, that the plant known as "skipping child," which grows in only one area on the planet of Thjeela, first sprang spontaneously from the footsteps of a little girl. The tale is told that after Khalista had selected a baby daughter, as was the custom of her tribe, she took the infant to the Holy Mother in Dartma for the traditional blessing. The Holy Mother held the child in her arms and asked Khalista her name.

"I will call her Marita after the flowers that used to bloom on the slopes of Mount Trayna, where we plan to live. I do not know why, but as she was being originated, I remembered a painting I once saw of one of these flowers. It was very beautiful, yet quite simple."

"Do you know what these flowers symbolized and why they no longer bloom?"

"I cannot remember . . . I think someone told me once, but I have forgotten. I hope I have not made a mistake. You have always taught us to honor the images of light we see in our minds."

"Yes, I have taught you that, and perhaps you have learned even more. Our history tells us that there was a time when Mount Trayna was covered with the marita blossoms. It did not matter whether the winter rains were abundant or did not come at all, in the spring the mountain came alive under the magnificence of these flowers.

Marita and Khalista on Mount Trayna

It was said you could not walk past one without feeling your heart fill with grace. I can remember as a young child hearing my great-grandmother talk about the last marita. This was also at the time when the last male had died, phased out through attrition, and our society had completed Simplification. The authorities placed the flower in a controlled environment where they worked to keep it healthy until such time as cuttings could be taken. It was hoped that these children of the last plant could eventually be reintroduced upon the slopes of Mount Trayna. But this was not to be. They all died quite rapidly when they were transplanted, and then finally the mother plant with them.

"The marita was not a complex flower. It did not have the startling size and perfect symmetry of a chrystalina. Nor did it have the enticing scent of an anneveria. In fact, it had no scent at all. What it had was absolute purity of intention."

"But why did they all die?"

"No one has ever been able to answer that question. But they have certainly tried. The Authorities organized numerous commissions to study the soil on Mount Trayna, the quality of the air, and even the psychological and social implications. But they were never able to agree on an answer."

"I want to do something to honor my union with my child, and it is my belief that the image of these flowers has some meaning for both of us. Perhaps if I were to study all the old reports, I could find the key to the disappearance of the flowers. I have some gift for understanding."

"Indeed you have a *great* gift. But what would this key give us?"

"Perhaps if we knew what went wrong we could take

steps to correct it. It might even be possible to generate facsimile seeds. Technology is far advanced from what it was then. Might this not be the answer?"

"You say that you wish to honor your union with this child, and yet these flowers will never come again in the form we remember them, for all we have now is legend. Your Marita lives today, and even if Mount Trayna remains forever barren, if you will give her the sweetness of your love, and your firm direction free of anger, and if you will nourish her without fear of the future, and accept her form and nature just as it is, the marita flowers will bloom again in your heart and in hers. And this will be the gift of honor you so long to give."

Marita lived with Khalista on the slopes of Mount Trayna, where her mother is considered to have founded the movement known as Inefficiency or "love without calculation." It is said to have had its inception when Khalista politely refused the Authorities' order to stop Marita's inefficient habit of skipping.

It is of course an historical fact that Marita grew up to be the first woman to give birth to a son in almost two hundred years. It is believed by some that upon the occasion of this natural birth, on the slopes of Mount Trayna, the skipping child began to blossom for the first time, a flower with beauty as affecting as the marita, and with a fragrance that is said to heal grief.

Your treasured opinions never made anyone happy.

PLANET: Sauv[10]

TRANSLATION: The primary industry on Sauv[10] is the codification of all mortal knowledge. Their encyclopedias, dictionaries, and other reference books are widely used in several galaxies. The long-term effect of this occupation on the Sauvits themselves has been to develop a deep neutrality regarding all intellectual issues. **"Facts are fashion,"** they say. And when someone is overheard insisting doggedly on his or her point of view, the typical Sauvit retort is, **"About even this, you will change your mind."**

MEANING: You cannot insist on being right and at the same moment extend the gift of love. The only punishable crime on Sauv[10] is narrow-mindedness, the penalty for which is to be a foster parent to a two-year-old and a parrot. The parrot is trained to say "I'm right" in a firm but cheerful voice forty-eight times a day, and the two-year-old is not trained to, but nevertheless does, say "No" in a firm but uncheerful voice to all attempts at communication. Despite their apparent skepticism regarding opinions, knowledge, and facts, Sauvits have cultivated an unreasonable love for all living things. Language is used carefully, not to achieve accuracy but to achieve compassion. Or, as the Sauvits themselves would put it: **An unloving question has no answer.**

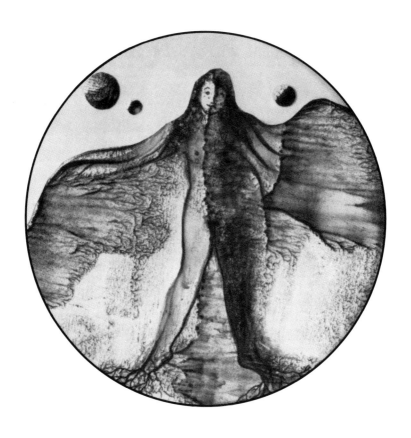

An angel spans two worlds

Asha the Lesser Angel

Behind the Coalsack, which blocks them from Earth's view, are twenty-three solar systems containing twenty-six inhabited planets. Although the stars are set apart, they have always seemed so randomly placed in the sky that, until recently, this constellation remained un-named.

Conflict has been a constant theme within each planet and, in modern times, among planets, even though the lesser angel Asha has been working to break this pattern since the inception of intelligent life. She has anointed a new prophet of peace every thousand years, but their teachings, no matter how simply expressed and faithfully lived by the prophets, have always been deeply misinter-preted and bitterly misused. Every decade she has sent a muse to inspire in some writer a new statement of truth, and although libraries throughout the constellation are now filled with pathways out of chaos, written in every style and language, they have had their moment among only a small percentage of readers. In recent centuries she has added to her efforts visions and revelations, which, when they first began, offered great promise. These miracles had profound effects on small segments of the populations and so Asha increased their frequency in an attempt to reach more people. Even if she had not done this, the results were inevitable. Ambitious individuals realized that they themselves could claim to have heard a message or seen a manifestation, and who was in a position to prove they had not?

Archangels have learned that true patience has no time limit, but many of the lesser angels have not, and as Asha became increasingly distressed over the enormity of the pain being experienced, she began casting about for still more ways of changing the basic nature of her charges. At about this time, Michasai, the oldest and wisest woman in the constellation, was now on her deathbed, and as she did with all who were ready to depart, Asha appeared before her.

She stood at the foot of Michasai's pallet and waited for the old woman to notice her, and when she did, Asha held forth her hands. "Do not be afraid, Michasai. I am here to go before you and behind you and to lead you on your way."

"I know you well, Asha. Since the time of my youth I have seen the gentle workings of your hands among my people and heard the reports of your influence from many other planets, and if you would think it arrogant of me to ask you a single question, I will go with you now without a word."

"I am here to serve you as well as watch over you," answered the angel, laughing like the sun. "I welcome anything you have to say!"

"Tell me then," said Michasai, "when I first looked at you, why were you not completely happy? I am at peace and ready to die, and yet I thought I saw a tear in your eye."

"Leave your body here for an instant and come with me," said Asha, "and I will show you the answer from a place where you can see it."

Together they journeyed to the tip of the Southern

Cross, from which Asha's constellation could be viewed in its entirety.

"How many wars can you see from here?" asked Asha. "How many murders? How many riots? How many rapes?"

"Even on one planet alone there are too many to count," replied Michasai. "And if I look at *all* the forms of cruelty, they blanket the planets like thick clouds of stinging insects."

"This is why I weep," said Asha. "This is why I have wept for a million years. I am a guardian and yet can find no means to change the hearts of my people to guard them from one another. You are the wisest of your people. Do you know of a way I have not tried?"

Michasai looked into the lovely eyes of the angel. "But, Asha," she said, "*I* have long since forsakened cruelty. Although it is not so bright as the fires of war, do you not see the glow of love that yet surrounds my dying body?"

Asha looked back to the old but comfortable pallet where the ancient body lay in rest. The tranquility of her features was so strong it could almost be touched, and indeed, now that she noticed, there was a slight glow within the simple room.

"And do you not see these same lights," continued Michasai, "—light of a different sort, light from both the living and the dying—sprinkled throughout your constellation?"

The angel looked and now could see them plainly. "Yes," she said, "and I suppose they were always there."

"I do not have the gifts of an angel," said Michasai. "Yet from my many years there is one thing I have learned: if I try to change those who do not wish change, I cannot love them with complete happiness. Yet if I step back in honor, I can remain their silent supporter—a friend even in their mistakes. And I have always believed that somewhere in their minds they can feel the alternative that my love offers, even if they are still too weak to accept it."

It is unusual for an angel to seek the wisdom of a mortal, and because of her great humility the holy seraphim elevated Asha to archangel. Soon thereafter planets throughout that quadrant of the galaxy began noticing that the twenty-three stars of her constellation did in fact have a definable form—that of a shimmering tree of light set like a jewel against the velvety darkness of the Coalsack. In a thousand years, when the particle cloud that is the Coalsack is scheduled to part, the Tree of Life constellation will be seen alongside the Southern Cross, and although the nature of Earth will not be transformed, those who are ready to behold it will look to the heavens and know that they are loved.

The Last Child of God

Circling the great sun Stalta is a single planet and nothing more. Although it has several names, so brilliantly does the planet shine in the vastness of space that within its galaxy it is known simply as "the eye of heaven." The people who inhabit it are unusual in that they have a single religion from which no group of detractors has ever split. Perhaps it is the simplicity of the teaching that has kept it beyond question, perhaps it is the small size and homogeneous nature of the population, or perhaps it is the religion's central concept itself. In the daily services only one reminder is given, that the world, and all the world of worlds, is over, and the power to harm has been removed. What is now before the eyes is mere replay, a final review of how it all ended. Thus the traditions of this religion contain no creation story, but only an ending story.

"The Story of Rest," as it is called, is about the final day when God was gathering His children into His house. There was still much to do because bringing to an end an entire cosmos with six island universes and so many galaxies that there are not numbers enough to count them is a complex task. But when God heard that there was still one person unaccounted for, He put aside all that He was doing. And immediately He began searching for His lost child.

In all the corners of the Outer World God looked, going to the depths of every black hole, entering the core of every star, sweeping clean the surface of every planet and asteroid. Knowing for certain that His child was not there, He then entered the Middle World, sixteen times as large as the Outer and still filled with the moaning gray forms of in-between emotions: boredom, discontent, lethargy, depression, and futility. Again He searched every corner and again He found nothing. Finally God entered the Under World where even now could be seen the last sharp roots of hatred, the broken webs of murder and deceit, the few remaining cinders of greed, and the final echoing screams of betrayal. There, tucked beneath a long shadow of guilt, He found His lost child.

God reached out His hand and said, "Why did you not come when I called you Home? Could you not feel my welcome?"

The lost child of God cowered and hid his eyes from the splendor of God's goodness. "There is no sin I have not committed," he said. "There is no mistake I have not made. I am not worthy to enter Your doors."

God answered: "It is not contrition that binds you, my child. It is not humility that hides you away. It is mere arrogance. Can you imagine an authority great enough to quench forever the happiness that I alone give? Do you think that what you have done can stop a life of which I alone am the source? Do you believe that you possess the power to harm even one small part of anything I have created? Surely you have suffered this illusion long enough. If there was a debt to be paid you have paid it. Now your family awaits you. Come and show them that I am so harmless, and so harmless is all that I have made, that you cannot even harm yourself."

And God returned Home with His child and set him gently down in his eternal place. And there went up an anthem of rejoicing that did not end.

Afterword

It has been suggested that Earth may be a kind of jail, or a planet of dropouts, or even hell itself. To believe this is not only to position Earth unfairly, but to assume the possibility of utopian planets peopled with entities that, although still retaining their separate bodies and separate minds, somehow live together in perfect unity. If you are feeling bad about ending up on Earth, please don't. It's about average.

With the burden of this knowledge—that throughout the cosmos there is no place entirely free of war, injustice, disease, and betrayal—I returned to Mervin and reported that I had completed my journey.

"Your journey is finished," said Mervin, "but is your quest complete? What of the bits and pieces of truth you were to look for?"

"They were there," I answered. "Within the heart of each one I found them."

"And was there any place in the cosmos where a part of truth was absent?"

"There was none," I said. "The whole is contained within the part, and even where the glimmerings of truth are very slight, Light itself resides in each one."

"Your journey is finished, your quest is complete, your answer is at hand. And yet you are not laughing! Is it, my beloved one, because you found no planet where bodies age until they reach the blossom of youth and then stay

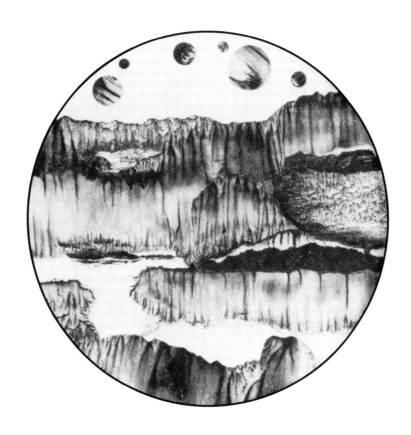

A landscape of Sei

frozen in time? Is it because you found no planet where, although everyone is different, they assign no value to their differences? Is it because you found no planet where there were degrees of openness, yet no degrees of deceit; where there were degrees of health, yet no degrees of illness; where there were degrees of wealth, yet no degrees of poverty; and where there were degrees of intimacy, yet no degrees of hate?"

"I found that everywhere there is a terrible struggle, and nowhere a complete rest."

"And do you know why this is?"

"I know that it need not be, for whether circumstances were favorable or unfavorable, I found those few who had relinquished struggle and knew a lasting peace."

"And for the many who know not peace, what do they struggle against?"

"They struggle against time; they battle it continually."

"Indeed that is the great and useless struggle. And the reason you do not laugh is that you are afraid they will not see through to its uselessness. But the other name for time is fear, and so that you will understand why, I will tell you the story of how time came to be.

"The first planet within the first universe was the planet of Sei. It was illuminated by twenty distant suns and twenty distant moons. The clouds of its sky danced with the colors of these heavenly bodies reflected off a million lakes and seas. Its softly shifting breezes carried the perfumes of forest flowers as tall as mountains, and carried too the life forms of Sei, for all of them had wings. This was the time of no time, the time before Time itself was conceded its present position of authority in the cosmos. And it was also the time when the people of Sei were very happy.

"Looked at from today, Sei would be thought of as a

backward planet. But the reason for its slow outward progress was that throughout the population there was a great love and respect for children. Industrializing the planet and building individual fortunes were low priorities for the simple reason that children did not think they were much fun. Wars were undreamed of. Hunger was never ignored. Parents flew carefully and kept their wings strong and safely trimmed. And, naturally, there was no crime or mind-altering indulgences because their effects on children are so obvious. Happiness was assured because there was a single guiding purpose, and just as any purpose based on love will do, it extended to all lesser priorities.

"From a distance, the planet looked somewhat like an apple because of the large indentation at its top. A comet had once collided with the polar sand cap and its heat had created a glass lake so large that the entire population of Sei could easily play on its surface. This expanse of glass was in fact the only mirror on the planet, and Mirror Lake's smooth warm surface lent itself to hundreds of amusements, like gliding across the turbulence that rose from it in undulating waves, skating over its shining flats, and sliding down its gently sloping sides.

"Unknown to the people of Sei, every ten million years the moons and suns came into alignment, causing a complete solar eclipse. The night this occurred, the planet cooled so quickly that Mirror Lake cracked into a million pieces, and when the people came to play the next morning, there was much confusion about how to react. The children thought the change was wonderful and immediately began running around looking for the funniest reflections, or spinning the shining pieces like tops, or building forts out of the mirrored blocks.

"But many of the adults began wondering if the cracks were a warning from some higher authority. Then suddenly one of them looked up and gasped, for there, projected onto the single cloud that had always seemed to hover above the polar region, was an unusual pattern of light and shadow, a shifting reflection from a million mirrors. 'There it is!' he shouted. 'That *Face* is what caused it.'

"As the others stared they began to see the same image. 'What does It want from us?' they asked. 'If It broke Mirror Lake, could It not break the entire planet?'

"It seemed obvious to most that if the face had transformed Mirror Lake into pieces, it must have a purpose for those pieces. The adults began taking them from the children and examining them very carefully, because, obviously, the children did not realize what they were for.

"Before, the adults had been aware of themselves as individuals, but because they had always seen their reflections in the company of everyone else, they had placed no more importance in this evidence of their separateness than the evidence of separate waves formed out of the single body of an ocean. But now, because of the smallness of the pieces of glass, they could see only themselves alone, each an isolated person in a broken mirror.

"As they stared at these images, even though they did so side by side, each began to think how different he was, how special, how set apart from the others, and the desire started to grow within them to increase these differences.

"To change themselves would require time, for the fruits of change are always in the future. Therefore, the adults assigned one of their number to watch the great face of time that hung over them and to report back any fluctuations in its mood. Meanwhile they went their separate ways in pursuit of the changes that they now knew time demanded and only time could fulfill. Some embellished their intellects, others added to their homes, and still others ennobled their wings with ornaments. Periodically the watcher would run among them crying out: 'Time is short!' or, 'Time is flying!' or, 'Time is running out!' depending on what was happening to the cloud on which the face of time appeared. As each new portent was heralded, the adults became more serious and more deliberate, because it was now clear that the time they had left was not to be taken lightly.

"The children returned to their separate homes and became adjuncts to their parents' lives instead of their reason for living. Desperately needing time to fulfill themselves, adults no longer had time for pursuits that did not lead to future gain. Naturally, with as many goals as there were people, conflicts grew and betrayals became necessary, anger was at last seen as the shortcut to success, and aggression became more useful than love. Now the people of Sei knew to judge one another according to their past accomplishments or future prospects, and it was not long before its progress was so great that Sei was indistinguishable from any modern planet.

"And this, my beloved one, is how time became important, because time is nothing more than the promise or threat of change. And just as perfect love can only be found in the present, perfect change can only be sought in the future, where it is destined to remain.

"Although each planet has its own peculiar set of dynamics, the attitude that touches all planets and plays itself out again and again is the unshakable conviction that time is the ground of all being, that it is not only real but flows in the single direction of new to old, birth to death, and that it does so in an orderly fashion.

"The happy fact is that time is not absolute, it is not sequential, it is not even very important. Life on the planets is like a movie being run the wrong way. This is not to say that it would be better if people were born old and grew progressively younger. That would be equally distressing. It is the *mind* that instructs *itself* to run backward, and it does so because of its unwavering faith in time.

"Time is merely a picture of the children of God running away from home, of creation being undone, of happiness turning to fear, of simplicity turning to confusion, of laughter turning to grief, of oneness turning to separation. Although this picture plays itself out everywhere, it can be watched in complete innocence. It does not have to be taken to heart. Yet, taking time to heart is the great pastime of the planets."

"And why will the planets not continue in this pastime forever?" I asked.

"If a bucket is lowered into a well and is brought up empty, how many times must this process be repeated before it is seen that the well is dry?"

"Although the number of times would vary from individual to individual," I answered, "surely none could fail to recognize such an obvious fact eventually."

"Yes, my beloved one," said Mervin. "And you yourself have already found a few who no longer attempt to drink from the well of time. Like a cup being filled drop by drop, like an ocean being filled by a thousand rivers, like a heart being filled with the memory of God, to their numbers will be added every last one."